MW00944046

HIDDEN ENTITY

SWEETFERN HARBOR MYSTERY #14

WENDY MEADOWS

MAJESTIC
OWL
PUBLISHING LLC

CHAPTER ONE

T he Fright Night Halloween Party preparations were underway at Sheffield Bed and Breakfast, and the whole house bustled and brimmed with activity. Brenda walked through the downstairs to observe the creative and ghastly decorations that had been hung up for the bash. Her head housekeeper, Phyllis Pendleton, walked with her. They were not only employer and employee, but also very good friends.

"I think this year will be the best yet, Brenda," Phyllis said. "I am amazed at how artistic and creative Allie is with her designs."

She pointed up toward a fake body hanging upside-down. The figure dangled from the majestic chandelier in the sitting room. Its eyes were black, and trickles of fake blood seemed to flow between ridges on its face.

1

Overall, it was the eeriest prop Brenda's young reservationist had created to date.

"I agree. She gets better as the days go by. I hope she lands that scholarship for college. Sweetfern Harbor will present it at the end of the year."

They talked about Allie Williams for a few more minutes before meeting her in the front foyer. Allie was bent over the list of guests soon to arrive to spend a long weekend at the bed and breakfast.

"We're ready for them," Allie said, looking up with a smile. "I can't wait to meet the guests and get to know them."

Brenda Sheffield Rivers took a deep breath and tried to calm her excitement before the next onslaught of visitors to her bed and breakfast. This was the norm for the owner. Once dinner was served the first night, she could then relax. She complimented Allie on the decorations.

"Wait until you see what I did in the upstairs hallway on the second floor." Allie's eyes shined in the sunlight that permeated the foyer. "Wouldn't it be something if we had a huge storm to go along with the celebrations? It would be so spooky."

Brenda and Phyllis laughed and had to agree with her. They started for the stairs just as the front door opened and Allie greeted the first guests.

Lauren and Ryan Meyers were first to arrive. Both were outgoing and in their twenties. Their tan skin and fit bodies made it obvious to Allie that they were outdoors people. The two jested with the young reservationist as she checked them in.

Lauren jabbed Ryan. "Don't make a spectacle of yourself, Ryan. This lovely young lady won't appreciate your performances right now. She's trying to do her job."

Ryan projected a crooked grin at Allie. "She doesn't appreciate my attempts at comedy. What can I say? I'm a natural born performer." His sandy red hair and crystal blue eyes sparkling with wit and humor left no doubt in Allie's mind that he was an entertainer. She thought he probably liked to do comedy and asked him if he performed. "Sometimes. Hey, your Halloween Fright Night could be my venue. We jumped at the idea to come here once we saw the postings about your party. Word of this bed and breakfast has reached far."

"I can't wait for the party," Lauren said. "We love Halloween."

He and his wife looked around at the ornate architecture of the mansion and took in every detail. Allie noticed their interest and told them a little bit about the 1890s Queen Anne style building.

"I suppose we'll find out even more during the tour," Lauren said excitedly.

They were shown their room on the second floor. Allie heard their laughter as they dodged two of the animatronic twitching ghouls that she had positioned along the passage.

Jolene and Marcus King were next to arrive. Allie was momentarily distracted when she noted Jolene's exquisite willowy frame and pristine facial features. Both were very friendly.

"We are here specifically for your well-advertised Halloween bash," Jolene said in graceful tones. "I believe in the paranormal. Are there ghosts here?" she laughed, a brief musical sound. "Don't answer that. I've no doubt there are plenty of shadowy figures in this historic building."

"Pay no attention to her," Marcus said. He appeared older than his wife. His handsome darker features contrasted to Jolene's fair skin. "I'm here to go along on her imaginative trips, but don't count me in as someone who believes in ghosts and bumps in the night."

After they left for their room, Allie smiled to herself. This should be a fun time for everyone. So far, all guests had come for one reason, and that was to enjoy everything Halloween offered at Sheffield Bed and Breakfast. The next guest was a man who appeared to be in his early forties. His personality was pleasant.

"William Pendleton insisted I not miss Fright Night this

Halloween." Clive Wilson laughed in a deep tone. "I've known William many years. I've referred entertainers to him a number of times, some of whom he has managed to lure up to Sweetfern Harbor on occasion."

"You won't regret being here for our Halloween celebration. We go all out to give everyone a good time." Allie noted the absence of a wedding band on the man's hand when he signed the guest registry book. Allie invited him, as she had the others, to gather for refreshments when he was settled in. "We hope everyone will join us in the sitting room on their first evening to get acquainted and enjoy some light refreshments." She gestured toward the large sitting room that opened through the ornate wooden archway across the hall. He thanked her and followed the porter Michael up the stairs to his room.

Brenda joined Allie, who updated her on the arrivals so far. "I'm glad they are all ready for a good time. The decorations upstairs and down are perfect, Allie. Let me know when Jenny gets here with the bouquets of fall flowers. That will put the finishing touch on everything."

"Is she still working at her shop? I hope she doesn't go into labor while she's arranging flowers."

Brenda smiled. "I suppose she will know when it's time. She isn't working her usual long hours, so I think she's planning to get some time to rest before the baby arrives."

Brenda was very proud of her stepdaughter, the capable owner of Jenny's Blossoms. She and her detective husband Bryce Jones were expecting their first child. Jenny was someone Brenda felt very lucky to know, and she regarded her as her own daughter.

"Your mother called a little while ago," Brenda told Allie. "She's bringing Halloween cakes and goodies over in a few minutes. It's a good thing Sweet Treats isn't next door. I'm obsessed with her new ginger spice cupcakes!"

"I know," Allie said with a roll of her eyes, "I think I'd eat one for breakfast every day if she let me. After I leave here, I plan to stop by her shop to go over her final baking plans for tomorrow night's big party, Brenda. Do you have anything you want to add?"

"I fully trust Hope. Thanks for your help in going over the plans with her, Allie. My hands are full right now."

They were interrupted when melodious voices flowed through the entryway as the front door opened. A woman in her forties appeared ahead of her friend who followed her. The first woman was well-coiffed and more sedate than the second one. Both wore friendly smiles.

"My name is Grace Mitchell," said the second woman, who was more bubbly, "and this is Karina Harris. We've come for a real diversion and hear Fright Night will do it for us." The two women shared a wink and a giggle.

Allie assured them they had come to the right place.

Brenda welcomed them and said she would see everyone a little later for refreshments. She left the group knowing that this weekend would be perfect. Every guest so far was eager to engage in all the activities. Her husband Mac would be surprised that Brenda had no doubts about it when he got home. Usually, Detective Mac Rivers expected to need to reassure his wife on the first night of new guests. He learned to accept her nervousness until she was sure things were going as smoothly as possible.

When Mac came into the bed and breakfast earlier than usual, he stood back and admired the transformation of the place. He helped his daughter carry in baskets of fall foliage and brilliant mums and asters. Brenda noticed the circles under Jenny's eyes.

"Join us in the sitting room, Jenny. You look like you could use a good break."

Jenny smiled. "I do become more tired each day. Dad, will you carry the rest of these baskets in? I'll take Brenda up on that invitation if it's alright with you."

"Take care of yourself, Jenny," Mac said, hurrying to take Jenny's baskets from her. He worried about his daughter, who was such a hard worker.

"Bryce tells me that often, Dad. I think this will be my last full week at the flower shop. I'll go in only when I feel up to it. Right now, I can barely see my feet."

When all were gathered together, Brenda asked everyone

to introduce themselves to the other guests. None had a problem, and lively conversation flowed through the room, though Karina Harris waited until she'd gathered a little more courage to speak to the group.

"I'm a researcher in the field of Alzheimer's disease. We're trying hard to find the source of the effects of it." Several commented on this, and Karina relaxed.

Grace mentioned that she was recently widowed. "Karina and I have been good friends since elementary school. We both needed a getaway. I work with her in the same research facility."

Clive Wilson kept his background brief. He stated William Pendleton encouraged him to see what a real party at Sheffield Bed and Breakfast had to offer. Phyllis spoke up and mentioned William was her husband. A few words back and forth about how she met him late in life and was now happily married drew others into the conversation.

Marcus King introduced himself and his wife Jolene. He told them he kept busy climbing the ladder in a large industrial business started by his grandfather. "Jolene works in finance in a bank in New York City. And, by the way, if you haven't heard already, she believes in hauntings and ghosts. She hopes to fulfill her desire to meet some of them here."

Everyone laughed, and Jolene was nonplussed. She gave

a tiny little smile and didn't hold back as she discussed her beliefs in the paranormal.

Grace stated that she, too, believed in the paranormal. "I have had sessions with a very good medium...since the passing of my dear husband. I didn't know what to think at first, but let me tell you, there is definitely more around us than most people are aware of."

She was the only one who ventured to tell a personal story other than Jolene. The financial advisor explained she had met with a psychic once while in college. "She knew things that only I knew. She told me she saw my mother standing over my shoulder. I believe she truly did. When I left her, I felt very close to my mother again."

Marcus listened as if he had heard her story many times before. Brenda was sure he had, since his wife told it like it was second nature to her.

"Are there spirits here, Brenda?" Marcus asked good-naturedly. Jolene looked at him in surprise.

"I'm not sure about that, but I suppose the Halloween lantern tours may tell a different story." Brenda was accustomed to guests asking that question. She had never seen ghosts roaming the halls of Sheffield Bed and Breakfast, but it made a good tale for Halloween, and she didn't like to disappoint the fanciful imaginations of her guests. She and Phyllis, along with Allie, had their ghost stories ready. The ambiance of the 1890s Queen Anne mansion gave them plenty of ideas.

When the subject was momentarily exhausted, all eyes switched to Lauren and Ryan Meyers. Lauren pulled her husband back down to his chair, signaling him to introduce them. He laughed and told his audience his wife was probably afraid he was going to come up with an elaborate comedy routine to make their introductions.

"I'll save the entertainment for the party. Lauren and I are big on the outdoors. We do a lot of hiking in the Rockies on vacations and we really like winter sports. We are from Minnesota."

"Yes," Lauren agreed with a smile. "Though we do love tackling adventures in every season. But my favorite pastime of all is to enjoy big holidays. Halloween is my absolute favorite. That's why we are here."

"Well, you're all in for a treat. We have invited about forty-five guests to the party," Brenda said. "We try to limit the number so that everyone has room to move around freely and enjoy themselves. Tours will open at ten tomorrow night. Everyone will be invited to enjoy our Halloween treats. That's when many more people will walk through." She explained they would be guided in small groups and to expect many suspenseful surprises along the way. She turned to Jolene. "You never know when a ghost will suddenly appear before you. Prepare yourselves to be frightened throughout Fright Night."

Some of the guests remained in the sitting room and others meandered through the lower floor admiring the artwork and Halloween decorations along the walls and up to the high ceilings. Brenda answered questions others had about the bed and breakfast mansion.

"How did you come to run this magnificent place, Brenda?" Clive asked.

"My uncle, Randolph Sheffield, left it to me. He was in theatre for many years. He came to Sweetfern Harbor several times to perform and was drawn to this place. It was abandoned and in disrepair at the time, but he was determined to purchase it and left his acting career to start a business as a hotelier. He spent several years restoring it down to the last detail."

"And what about his family?" Jolene said. She realized her implication. "I don't mean you aren't his family or that you didn't deserve it, but I'm just curious where his wife or children are now. I can't imagine wanting to leave this place."

"He never married, and he had no children. My parents and I visited here once when I was a child. He showed me the antique toys in the attic, and I played there for hours while my parents visited. I was an adult when he passed away, and I had not seen him for many years. Later, listening to my father's stories of their childhood, I realized the toys must have belonged to him and Randolph. Uncle

Randolph kept them all those years. He loved children."

"That is so touching," Jolene said.

"He was a wonderful, charismatic man. I was shocked to learn he left Sheffield House to me, actually. He had established it as a bed and breakfast, but I didn't know much about it. I lived in Michigan and worked as an assistant to a private investigator." She laughed at her memories of arriving in Sweetfern Harbor. "I wasn't sure I could run something like this at first. I soon came to love it, and since I arrived, I've never left."

"It is just beautiful," Jolene said. "You were lucky to inherit such a treasure. Who knows if it would have been abandoned again if you hadn't moved here?" The group agreed with her.

"We'll never know how things would have turned out otherwise," Brenda said. "I've come to love the life of a bed and breakfast owner, and I love this town, too. Everyone is very friendly here, and I feel like I now have a huge family. My father even moved to Sweetfern Harbor, too. He married my chef a month ago."

Brenda was happy to have an audience to listen to her happy words, but then worried she was talking too much. She excused herself gracefully and told them she would see them at seven for dinner. Several said they wanted to hear more stories about her Uncle Randolph's restoration process and his background in theatre. She promised them she would tell them everything they wanted to know later.

"Wait until after the tours...you may learn more during them." She grinned mysteriously. Just then, Mac Rivers arrived in the hallway, the perfect excuse for her to step away from her guests, many of whom began to return to their rooms to relax before dinner.

She linked arms with Mac, and they headed down the back pathway to their cottage on the grounds. Mac smiled when Brenda sighed deeply.

"I take it the guests are all to your satisfaction," he teased.

"I am really looking forward to this weekend. By tomorrow night, everyone will be more than happy they chose this weekend. Let's have some tea before dinnertime." They entered their little cottage together and settled in to talk.

In the front hallway of the bed and breakfast, Phyllis busied herself with a few last tidying tasks. Then her eyes lit up when William walked in. Her husband hugged her and asked if he could do anything to help.

"I believe everything is ready. I'm not sure about tomorrow night. You may want to come early if you want to help make sure things are in order." Phyllis smiled adoringly at her husband. "Clive Wilson has checked in. I think he went to his room. Do you want to see him?"

William was indeed anxious to see his old friend. Clive had been devastated the last time he saw him. William convinced him to come to the Sheffield's party to have a good time and forget his troubles. Months ago, his friend Clive had discovered that his wife was in love with someone else. To Clive's surprise, she left him with few words except to tell him she had already filed for divorce. To this day, Clive remembered being numb with shock that day, a feeling that stuck with him for a long time. When he and William had last met up in Boston, Clive said he had had no idea troubles between him and his wife had been building to that degree.

William had only told Phyllis a little bit of this, however. He hesitated at her offer to go knock on his room door to see if he was available to talk. "I think I'll see him tomorrow morning. He may want to breathe in the relaxing Atlantic salt air and enjoy the tranquility first. Are you finished here? I have reservations for us tonight at the Italian bistro, your favorite place."

Phyllis gave Brenda a quick call to let her know she was leaving. Then she and William headed for home to get dressed before dinner. The Pendleton mansion on the hill overlooking the ocean and the town of Sweetfern Harbor still took her breath away. It had taken a few months for her to accept that this place was truly her home. William encouraged her to redecorate it any way she liked, and Phyllis soon found ways to tone down the formality of it.

14

After the sitting room and front entryway of the bed and breakfast emptied out of new guests, Allie started to close the office and prepare to leave for the evening. She checked in with one of the housekeepers who remained to see that guests had everything they needed until dinnertime.

Footsteps came hurrying down the main stairs toward the front desk. "I can't believe we were so lax," Grace Mitchell said in a rush. She hurried up to Allie. "Is there a costume shop in town? We totally forgot to bring our costumes."

"Don't worry about that. We have an entire room filled with costumes for our guests to use. You know about Randolph Sheffield's theatre background? Well, he left behind a number of wonderful vintage pieces, and Brenda has also had other items tailor-made—cloaks and masks and things like that. I'm sure you will find something to wear. I can show you to the costume room now, or I can meet you in the morning to give you a tour of what we have to offer."

Relief spread across Grace's face. "Tomorrow morning will be fine. Thank you so much."

Allie started to pick up her purse after Grace left when she heard other voices on their way down to the first floor.

"I am sure there are plenty of secret rooms and passageways in this place," Jolene said.

"You could be right, but Brenda did say she didn't know of any." Marcus King displayed plenty of patience with his wife. They greeted Allie on their way outside. "The fall air is just the right temperature," Marcus said. "We're going to take a stroll before dinner."

Karina Harris and Grace Mitchell also opted to go for a walk along the ocean before dinner. The other guests scattered to find their own interests, and the bed and breakfast grew quieter. Allie only heard the muted clattering of pans from the kitchen in the rear and she breathed in the scents of dinner.

Allie started for the back door where her car was parked. She stuck her head in the kitchen and told Chef Pierre goodnight. On her way, she saw Brenda and Mac walking together along the paths through the mum garden and waved at them. Brenda told her they would see her in the morning.

The bent figure darted along the tree line and into the woods, unnoticed.

CHAPTER TWO

J olene was beautiful at age twenty-nine. She was aware of her fine features and yet didn't flaunt it in front of others. She preferred to build on her career assets. She worked hard at the large New York City bank that employed her and was pleased to be recognized for her professional acumen rather than her looks. She had received plenty of offers to model as a teenager and a young woman and had turned down every one. She loved working with numbers and exceled in popularity with clients and investors as a star financial advisor.

The day Marcus walked into the bank, she was drawn to him immediately. Marcus King was a handsome dark-haired man in his mid-thirties. He carried himself well. She heard him ask her supervisor for the best financial advisor they had, and she found him sitting across from her. He preferred to approach her professionally, but it proved hard for him to retain that stance. Jolene asked pertinent questions in the same manner. She discovered he was an important man in the business world. He held the position of CEO of a well-known industrial company.

They clicked right away, and he hired her. By the end of that first session with Jolene, he offered her a job in his company. She declined. It had taken her a long time to build her reputation where she was. In the end, he knew it was fruitless to try to convince her. Instead, he decided to ask her out to dinner.

Jolene and Marcus fell deeply for one another. She liked to have fun outside work, and he went along with her likes. There was something alluring about her, especially when she threw herself completely into holiday parties. Halloween was no exception. Even her belief in ghosts and the paranormal fascinated him.

Now that they were married, he had picked the perfect getaway for them in Sweetfern Harbor, specifically Sheffield Bed and Breakfast. He knew the annual Halloween celebration at the bed and breakfast was widely renowned among those interested in such things. Jolene was thrilled when he showed her their reservations.

Even Marcus was caught up in the enthusiasm displayed by the other guests who checked in. He felt Jolene's light tap on his arm before they had entered the sitting room earlier.

"I think I know that woman," she said. Marcus looked at the person she referred to. "I'm sure her name is Lauren. Seth Hill was in love with her and they were ready to marry." Marcus asked why they hadn't. "His mother is an overbearing woman. She told everyone wild stories about Lauren's family. I don't recall exactly what since I didn't care for Mabel Hill at all. She didn't want her son to marry someone 'like that,' in her words."

"She is happily married now, it seems," Marcus said.

Lauren laughed with Ryan across the room and Jolene could see Lauren was happy with her choice. The more she talked with Lauren during the gathering, the more Jolene felt Seth lost out.

Lauren knew Jolene eyed her closely at times and was uncomfortable under her scrutiny. She finally turned to the woman next to her and decided to be blunt.

"I feel you are staring at me for some reason. Have we met?" Lauren asked.

A slight flush flooded Jolene's face. "I'm sorry. I'm sure we met a few years ago. Did you attend a party at the Rockhill Country Club with Seth Hill?"

Lauren found it hard to swallow the last bite she had taken. When she recovered, she nodded in the affirmative. "I knew Seth at the time, and we dated...but that was before I found Ryan." She turned to her husband and squeezed his arm happily.

"I'm happy you found the right one," Jolene said. She had the grace to change the subject. "Do you believe in the paranormal?"

Lauren laughed. "I suppose there is such a thing, but I've never come across any ghosts. Maybe I will during the party. We're looking forward to a ghost tour. I hear they offer one through all the rooms that are creepy in this place."

"I'm hoping to encounter some. I'm sure there are secret rooms and hidden passageways here." Jolene leaned forward. "In fact, I was sure I heard something moving around behind the hallway wall."

Marcus chuckled. "You've said that before about hidden rooms, Jolene, and I hope for everyone's sake, you stumble across one or two ghosts. At least let's hope it's not mice in the walls!" Everyone laughed at this.

She and Lauren edged closer and spoke in low tones. "I think Clive is a bachelor," Lauren commented. "I don't see a wedding ring, do you?" Jolene nodded in agreement. "Maybe he's one of those types who travels in hopes of finding his soulmate."

Jolene laughed aloud at that moment. Everyone's eyes landed on her. She waved her hand to indicate she didn't mean to be so rude. All resumed their conversations and Jolene spoke in a hushed voice to Lauren. "Perhaps he'll take a ghost home." Both women covered their mouths to stifle their next outburst.

After the initial meeting between the guests, Jolene latched onto Marcus's arm and they headed for the waterfront. They talked about the amiable group of fellow guests and agreed they chose the best weekend to be there. They took deep breaths of the bracing autumn air and listened to the ocean waves.

Lauren relaxed once she realized Jolene wasn't there to criticize her. She wondered if Jolene knew about her past. If so, she seemed like a mannered woman who was not the type to bring up difficult subjects among strangers. For now, Lauren and Ryan focused on the celebration set for the next night. Lauren buried the past once again. It had been some time since she had come so close to reliving it.

Clive Wilson enjoyed small gatherings over finding himself in the middle of a large crowd. He liked the intimacy of the bed and breakfast. William had been right. He needed to get away and do something entirely different from his everyday life. Teaching at New York University tended to lock him into a boring routine at times. He had no idea what awaited him when it came to a celebration at Sheffield Bed and Breakfast. Phyllis and William were certainly caught up in it all. He smiled to himself when he recalled the earlier conversations. He didn't doubt there were things the ordinary person didn't sense when walking through the world, but he was a practical man. To believe in ghostly things floating around old buildings was the farthest from his reasoning. Still, he had no problem with others who did believe in such things. After all, it was Halloween and to be expected.

Before everyone left the sitting room earlier, Clive felt he had a kinship with them all. Brenda had made him feel welcome and offered ideas of how he could spend his time while visiting her bed and breakfast.

"Shops are open downtown until nine each night," Brenda told him. "It is a short walking distance if you're up for a stroll." He smiled at her. "Or the ocean is right here." Brenda pointed in the direction of the steps down to the beach area.

They both turned when they heard William's voice. He invited Clive to join him in the gardens. The two friends caught up with one another until Clive went inside for the first dinner of his visit. William and Phyllis decided to walk in the crisp air to the restaurant.

The dinner at the bed and breakfast had proven to be lively, with conversation and good food. Clive breathed deeply and relaxed as he entered into conversations that had nothing to do with students or academia. Brenda answered a few questions about the bed and breakfast. No one mentioned the paranormal again.

As Sheffield Bed and Breakfast closed down that night, Clive Wilson knew he would sleep soundly. William had promised him before his arrival to take him around town, and that would be a good activity for the next day. His old friend William Pendleton was a different man now that he was married to Phyllis Lindsay, Clive reflected. He remembered how William's former wife had held a tight rein on him before her sudden death a few years ago.

When Brenda and Mac reached their cottage, they were ready to turn in for the night.

By morning, clouds began to move in and then recede to allow the sun to peek through.

The staff at Sheffield Bed and Breakfast busily took care of last-minute details in anticipation of the party set to begin at six in the evening. The invitations to the guests in town encouraged everyone to entertain the party with creepy creations and costumes. There would be judges, and whoever won best entertainer would be presented with a free weekend stay at the bed and breakfast.

Brenda walked to the kitchen and conferred with Chef Pierre.

"I have everything in order, Brenda. Taste this stuffed pepper filling." Brenda took a whiff of the fragrant, herb-roasted meat filling and then laughed aloud when she saw how he had carved the green and orange peppers into jack-o-lantern faces. She tasted the meat mixture and approved. "I will serve these eerie snakes as well." A line of curvy, buttery dough snakes lay on baking sheets ready to go in the oven. She could tell her chef was thoroughly enjoying himself when he presented the snake-shaped calzones. "I have even more concoctions that I think your guests will love."

"I don't doubt that at all, Pierre. You have some great ideas. The tables will be set up and ready right at six this evening. We'll have the entertainment contest after dessert. Judges are going to pick the best costume, too. Then the tours will begin."

Brenda and Pierre were startled when they heard the clap of thunder. Lightning flashed across the wide kitchen window.

"It looks like we'll have a spooky night with this storm coming in," Pierre said.

"I really hope it isn't short-lived. I'd like it to continue during the party and tours." Brenda peered through the window and noticed a clearing in the sky that appeared as fast as the storm had. "I'm going to look at the weather report and see if more is coming later. Maybe this was just a prelude."

"A real storm would certainly add to the atmosphere," Pierre said.

The chef smiled at his boss. It proved easy for him to get into the mood of every event Brenda hosted at the bed and breakfast. This was no exception. Then he remembered something. "By the way, Brenda, have you had an exterminator inspect the premises recently? I'm convinced I'm hearing some kind of scratching in the wall near the back stairs. I wonder if a squirrel or other small animal has found its way inside."

"I hope not. I have the building inspected yearly to make sure there are no openings anywhere so that won't happen." She asked her chef to tell her exactly where he heard the noise. Pierre showed her. The wall appeared solid. They walked outside and looked for any openings and found none. "I'll have the inspector come back out and make sure."

At the front desk, Allie was excited about the continuing preparations for the party. She met Karina and Grace as they came from the dining room. "I'm ready to take you to the costume room whenever you are. Just let me know when."

"We're ready now," Grace said.

Allie led them to the end of the hallway on the second floor and opened the double doors leading into the large room that she and Brenda had decorated especially for costume selection. The guests gasped at the lavish fabrics and stunning dresses hanging from the racks. An antique three-way mirror gleamed at one side of the room, and a changing room awaited behind curtains nearby.

"I guess our choices will prove harder than we imagined," Karina said.

Allie agreed there were plenty of ideas to choose from. She showed them groups of costumes arranged according to era and themes. "This collection features traditional Halloween costumes, creepy and spooky themes, but any that you see are acceptable to wear for the party. It's the time of year to be whatever you want to be!"

Grace turned to her friend. "We'd better pick carefully. I mean to win the costume contest tonight." They laughed like schoolgirls, and Allie joined them.

"I think I'll choose this one. I can be the crimson countess," Karina said, touching the rich velvet brocade of a dress that swooped to the floor. She stepped back and shook her head. "It may be too fitted, though."

"Take that one," Grace insisted. "You have the figure for it. And that tone of red will be perfect for you." She looked through the rack. "What do you think about the cat girl costume?"

Karina laughed. "It is just like you to choose that one. Take it and we'll pick out our masks and accessories. What are you going to be tonight, Allie?"

"I'll tell the two of you but no one else. I chose to be a ghost maiden. I'll wear all white and the dress is handkerchief-style. I have the perfect white mask with sparkles on it and a plumed headpiece." Allie felt better after telling someone about her choice. She wanted it to be a surprise, but she was so excited about the outfit she had chosen that she wanted to share her secret.

Karina and Grace put the costumes in their room while Allie waited to accompany them downstairs. They chatted about performing. Karina told them she was drawing the line at that category.

"I'm definitely no performer, and besides, I would freeze up on the spot in front of all those people."

The bed and breakfast buzzed more than usual that morning, which promised a great night ahead.

Lauren and Ryan Meyers pulled out their costumes to make sure they were pressed and ready. One of the housekeepers had ironed the wrinkles out.

"I don't know why you chose to be a zombie, Ryan." Lauren shook her head but couldn't hide her smile.

"I like the way zombies walk. I have my act ready for tonight. Are you getting up there to try for a prize, Lauren?"

"I doubt I can compete against you, Ryan." In truth, she had no desire to perform. "I'm counting on you to win. I want to come back soon. Don't you think it's the perfect getaway? This place is wonderful."

"It is for sure. If I win, we should come back in the summertime. I hear they are famous for the sailboat races around Independence Day in July. We could do some sailing, too."

They talked about things they read in the brochures that detailed year-round events in Sweetfern Harbor.

"We have to get through this big celebration and then plan to come back for others," Lauren said. Adrenaline raced through them while they donned their costumes.

In the bustle of preparations, guests and staff passed through the hallways all day long. Perhaps because of the noisy excitement, no one heard any more faint noises from behind the walls of the hallway, except for Chef Pierre, who made a note to talk to Brenda again once the big party was over. Fright Night kept him busy, and there was no time to stop and investigate the rodents any further.

It was late afternoon when Hope Williams came through the back door laden with Halloween treats catered from her bakery. Pierre greeted her and sent two of his assistants to retrieve the rest from her van. She told him she was going to find Brenda and check on Allie, too.

Brenda met her in the hallway near the kitchen. Hope admired the décor that had changed the usually sunny and friendly-looking bed and breakfast into a spooky, dramatic scene perfect for the Halloween party. She was proud of Allie.

"It looks like another storm is brewing out there, Brenda. I wanted to get everything delivered before an onslaught of rain."

Allie Williams chatted with a few guests, and when she heard her mother's voice, she joined the women. "I hoped we'd have a storm tonight," she said. "This will be a perfect Halloween. I have the lanterns cleaned and ready, Brenda. They are in your office."

Brenda thanked her. "I feel good about everything. This will be our best yet. And I'm so glad we have guests who are so enthused, too."

"To say nothing of everyone from Sweetfern Harbor who's coming," Hope said. "All the shop owners have lined up extra staff to take over while they are here at the party. Molly offered to bring more coffee if you need it, Brenda."

Brenda assured her they were ready, and she wanted those who worked so hard downtown to simply bring themselves. She looked forward to a night celebrating with her friends and fellow business owners. With her friends and her staff by her side, the night would be simply perfect.

CHAPTER THREE

While guests donned their costumes, Brenda and Mac walked through the main floor. Mac was impressed with the way the décor turned out. Lights were dimmed to a soft glow and they took a last look at the dining room. Chatter from the foyer reached them, and Brenda took a deep breath.

"Are you ready, Detective?" she asked her husband.

"I am if you are, Mrs. Rivers," he replied, lifting her hand to kiss her fingers like the gentleman that he was. With a happy smile, Brenda and Mac went to their cottage to get dressed, too.

Mac and Brenda opted to dress in Victorian garb. Mac's old-fashioned three-piece suit had long tails and made him look like a gentleman detective or a duke from old England. Brenda's dress, bordered with satin ribbon, fell in beautiful rich colors down to the hoop skirt. Before greeting the first partiers, they positioned their masks. By the time they walked together to the main house, everyone seemed to be arriving at the same time, and Brenda jumped right into her hostess duties.

"Please, enjoy yourselves and mingle. Dinner will be served in the main dining room. There are tables set up also on the veranda. I hope you all have a frightfully enjoyable evening," Brenda said with a little wink.

When the crowd of guests had all arrived from town and the bed and breakfast's overnight guests had descended in their costumes, the variety of costumes created a stunning display of colors in the spooky gloom of the lighting. Guests swayed to the background music with cups of sparkling blood-orange punch in hand. When Chef Pierre and his assistants announced the dinner, everyone marveled at the inventive Halloween-themed food, from the snake stromboli to the jack-o-lantern stuffed peppers. The crowd favorite was the miniature sausages Pierre had wrapped in narrow strips of flaky pastry to look like mummy fingers. Everyone got a kick out of the creativity of the feast, and after they were happily stuffed, the crowd mingled in the sitting room and the formal living room, enjoying the music.

Once the party was in full swing, attention was drawn to the delectable desserts paraded out on massive silver trays. Allie grinned to see her mother's sweet treats being admired by everyone. There were miniature jelly tarts designed to look like monster eyeballs and chocolate spiderweb brownies, and everyone raved over the flavor of the lemon meringue cupcakes with little ghost faces and red velvet cupcakes with red licorice devil horns.

Allie and Phyllis took turns selecting classic Halloween songs for the party to enjoy until the small band they hired was ready. Eerie tunes floated throughout the bed and breakfast until it was time for the entertainment competition.

The double doors opened wide between the sitting room and the dining room and the first entertainer walked to the front of the crowd. He was a manager at the local bank. He bowed and then proceeded to perform a few impressive magic tricks with his wife as his assistant. Everyone clapped. The next few performers also showed considerable talent, and the panel of judges consulted after each one in low whispers.

"What number are you, Ryan?" Lauren asked.

"I'm up next." Ryan wobbled in his zombie gear, legs and arms stiffened to emphasize his role. "I have the scariest performance of all of them." He grinned behind his mask when his number was called.

Lauren shivered when she saw the fake knife in his hand. Her husband was talented when it came to entertainment, but she wished he had chosen something else. Memories shot through her mind of the last time she saw someone walking with a real knife in hand. The party around her faded as the memory overtook her senses. She had watched in fascination and horror as the figure walked beneath her window and onto the neighbor's lawn. Even through the closed window, she heard the frantic voice calling out, followed by moans as he crumpled to the ground. The more her memories flooded over her, the more she sank deeper within herself. The laughter in the room jolted her back to reality.

She shook her head and tried to focus on her husband, the entertainer, capering at the front of the room for everyone's amusement and telling zombie jokes. She meant to tell Ryan everything about her early teen years, but after Seth Hill, her first love, rejected her, she didn't want to risk losing Ryan, too. She was convinced that after Seth's affluent parents learned the truth about her, they must have threatened Seth with something that meant more to him than she did. It terrified her to think that the truth about her might scare away Ryan one day, too.

However, she realized, perhaps if Ryan did know her story, he wouldn't have dressed as a zombie and carried a knife with him. Or perhaps, she thought with a sinking feeling, they would never have married and come to Sheffield Bed and Breakfast to begin with. Her mind jerked back to reality again when she saw the audience draw back from the zombie as he awkwardly made his way through the crowd nearest the front.

He pretended to slash everyone as he walked stiffly among them. Each pulled back in fear and then laughed as he passed them by. His demeanor came across to his wife as a crazy man in a frenzy. Lauren took small breaths in quick succession and drew back. Ryan's eyes caught hers and something made him smoothly end his performance. Everyone clapped as he made his way back to her side.

"Are you all right, Lauren? You seemed shaken." Ryan chuckled. "I guess that means I really am a better actor than I thought. I'm sure you and I will be back here for that free weekend after all."

Lauren smiled faintly. Ryan was distracted as those around them told him how convincing he had been during his act.

From across the room, Brenda watched the pair and she, too, noticed genuine fear in Lauren's eyes. It lasted briefly, but long enough for Brenda to note it. She edged toward the couple and congratulated Ryan on his performance. Lauren had removed her mask and wiped her brow with her sleeve before she returned it to cover most of her face. In that fleeting moment, Brenda noted she was paler than usual.

"Are you all right, Lauren?" Brenda said. "It is a little

warm in here with all of these people. We can get you something cool to drink."

Ryan voiced his concern. Lauren agreed with a nod to Brenda and followed her to the buffet. Brenda assured Ryan she would get something cold for Lauren. She insisted he return to his new fans. Lauren chose a cold glass of orange punch.

"Ryan should go into acting as a career," Brenda said.

"That is something he has always loved, but he has said that he must make a living and he's not sure we can manage it. It would take some time for him to become good enough."

They chatted for a few minutes until Brenda was certain she could pose another question without seeming to intrude. "Lauren, you looked upset during the last part of Ryan's act. I'm curious what it was that unnerved you."

Lauren assured Brenda she felt fine. "You were right about how warm the room was getting. I think that's what hit me. I did feel a little faint. I'll finish this glass of punch and then find Ryan. I know you have plenty to do, Brenda. Don't worry about me."

After the hostess left, Lauren thought about Ryan's love for her. She wished now that she had told him long ago about the horror she witnessed at age fourteen. Ryan once hinted about having children, but she avoided speaking about it, even though he still occasionally mentioned the topic. That was the one thing she didn't want to risk, and she couldn't tell him why. Not yet. But most of all, she should have told him that her family member had been incarcerated in a mental hospital. She vowed to tell him the next morning. If he left her, she would have to deal with the consequences. She could no longer carry her hidden past in silence.

Her attention was drawn back to Ryan, who seemed to be searching for her. Their eyes met, and she hurried to his side just in time for the judges to announce he won the contest. He hugged her tightly before they walked to the judges' table to retrieve the gift card.

Brenda then announced the winner of the costume contest. Karina Harris blushed when she had to walk to the front of the crowd in her fitted crimson dress. She was presented with a generous gift card to be used in any of the shops in the downtown area of Sweetfern Harbor.

Chef Pierre and his assistants helped clear the leftover food from the main meal. They efficiently restored order to the dining room and spread clean orange and black tablecloths again over the tables. Pierre directed his staff to do the same in the attached veranda. Snacks and goodies from Sweet Treats were placed everywhere. The tables were laden with tempting delicacies.

A few of the bed and breakfast guests decided to retire for a brief respite in their rooms to freshen up. The Meyers hesitated and then decided they would do the same. Lauren wanted a quick shower before coming back downstairs for the late-night tours. Sweat clung to her body inside the heavy costume.

"I wouldn't worry about showering again, Lauren. With more of a crowd coming in, no one will notice." Ryan pulled his wife close to him and she joined in his laughter, though she still felt uneasy.

"I suppose you are right about that. I may as well finish the night like everyone else. I do want to wash my face, at least. It will help me cool down." Ryan nodded and took the key card out of his pocket to unlock their room.

When Lauren and Ryan opened their door, they stood frozen in shock. Their belongings had been moved. Not exactly ransacked—but something was clearly amiss. Their suitcases lay on the floor in front of the closet where they had been sitting neatly on luggage racks when they left for the party. Pillows on the bed slumped over the foot of the bed instead of neatly at the headboard as before. It appeared to be mischief rather than vandalism.

Lauren spoke first. "You don't think this is part of the Halloween shindig, do you?"

"Of course not. No self-respecting bed and breakfast would come in like this without our permission. I doubt Brenda and Mac would do something like this. It's strange that nothing has been destroyed...why scatter our stuff like this?"

"Who could have done it?" Lauren said. She pointed to her small jewelry case. It was opened, and her cherished pearl necklace looped over the side of it. "That's the necklace that Grandmother left my mother. After my mother died, it passed to me. Thank goodness it's still here, but surely it wasn't a thief if they didn't take it." Lauren shuddered. "I feel so vulnerable knowing someone handled such a precious object." Tears edged her eyelids.

Ryan put his arm around her and pulled her close. "Wait right here, Lauren. I'm going to find Brenda and Mac. Someone will answer for this. I'll leave the door open and be right back." He gave her a quick kiss. "Look around in case something else is missing. If you need to, go out to the hallway quickly and yell your head off if you have to."

While Ryan left to look for the owners, Lauren walked slowly around the room. She took a second look and saw a folded piece of paper that stuck out from beneath the jewelry box where her necklace had been moved. If she hadn't looked closely, the note was so small she might not have seen it at all. She snatched it up and read. "Seth is waiting for you." She crumpled the note in her sweaty palm and felt her heart beat fast. She dropped the wadded note when she heard Ryan's voice in the hall, returning.

"Nothing appears to be missing. But someone has been in our room. Look at it." He stood at the doorway and motioned for Brenda and Mac to enter ahead of him. "Someone has obviously invaded our privacy."

Lauren stood with her fists clenched. Her ashen face grew taut. Brenda hurried to her and told her to sit down for a few minutes to catch her breath.

"We will look into this," Mac said, his mouth set in a grim line. "Only Brenda has the master key card, and there are no extras other than the two you were given." Mac snapped photos of the initial disarray while he talked. Brenda quickly closed the guest room door, not wanting anyone to eavesdrop from the hallway.

Ryan opened his mouth to protest the lack of privacy once again until he noticed Lauren. He sat next to her on the bed and pulled her against him. "They will get to the bottom of this, Lauren. It's okay. Try to relax."

Mac called his fellow detective Bryce to join them from downstairs. Brenda secretly glanced at her watch. Tours would begin in less than five minutes. She assured the Meyers they were safe and promised to have someone stationed in the hallway to make sure no one else attempted to enter. "Maybe if you rejoin the party, it will take your mind off things for a while. In the meantime, the detectives will take your statements and gather any evidence they can find." Lauren thanked Brenda and she told Ryan they could do nothing at this point anyway.

Brenda breathed a sigh of relief. "I'll go back downstairs with you. Tours are almost ready to begin, and I'm in line to be the first tour guide."

Mac and Bryce remained in the room for a few minutes longer and then went downstairs and into Brenda's office off the foyer. Mac pulled Brenda aside just before the first tour was to begin. "This baffles me. Only the main room was in disarray and nothing in the bathroom. No signs yet of forced entry or anything stolen. Do you think the guests left the door unlocked by mistake and someone decided to prank them?"

"That could explain it, but something tells me there is more to it." Brenda glanced at her watch again and then felt Phyllis and Allie looking at her with impatience. "I have to get moving, Mac. It's time for the first tour." She thought about Mac's remarks. "I really do think something else is up. Only the overnight guests have been up to their rooms. I don't believe they would pull that kind of prank with the pending celebrations and all the people who are expected to be in the building."

"That makes sense, Brenda. I'll stay here with Bryce and we will lock it behind us until tours are over. I'll let you know if we find anything unusual or telling." He assured her he would have an extra plainclothes officer on the floor. "He can put on one of those costumes and he'll fit right in."

Brenda began to gather her first tour group and was

getting into the spirit of the Halloween party again when she heard a comment.

"I am sure I heard something through one of the walls on the second floor," Jolene King said. "I heard it when I walked down the hallway."

Marcus shook his head as onlookers took in everything she said. "Jolene, I'm sure it was just a room you were hearing. Perhaps in an old house like this, the walls are thin."

"That can't be it," Jolene said quietly, looking around her, adding, "I've been listening, and none of the rooms upstairs leak any sounds into the hallway. And the spot where I heard it? There's no room there that I could see."

"Maybe we'll hear it on one of the tours," a woman said excitedly.

"I'm going to be careful in case it jumps out in front of me." Her companion enjoyed the conspiracy theme and others went along with it.

Marcus frowned skeptically and muttered something about air vents and old pipes as the group got ready to follow Brenda on the tour.

Jolene had thoughts of her own. This was shaping up to be the best Halloween she had ever experienced. She would prove to everyone there was not only a hidden room, but a paranormal entity living in Sheffield Bed and Breakfast.

Brenda listened to the excited conversations and decided to use the story as a way to draw tourists in along the tour.

She deepened her voice when she turned to her group. "Is everyone ready to be scared out of your wits? Fright Night holds secrets you can't imagine. Keep your lanterns on, my friends. You never know what waits for you along the dark corridors of Sheffield House."

A few nervous giggles escaped from the tourists. The dimmed lights throughout the bed and breakfast were dimmed lower. When Brenda reached the third step on the stairs, she paused abruptly, her face tense as if listening to unknown sounds. Her face looked eerie in the faded light when she turned to her group. She shook her head in mock sorrow and then resumed her somber steps.

Phyllis and Allie commented they hoped to put on such an act for their groups as well. "Brenda's a natural. She really knows how to get everyone's attention," Phyllis said. She and Allie began to gather their groups.

As for William, he enlisted Clive Wilson's help with the arriving tourists who were beginning to form a long queue on the front porch and steps and pathway of the bed and breakfast. He explained that Mac and Bryce were called to an emergency and he needed someone to hand each visitor a number. Clive felt relieved to have a purpose and told visitors to hang on to their numbers.

"As soon as your number is called, your group will join one of the guides. In the meantime, enjoy refreshments and one another," he said, gesturing to the punch and cider and sweet treats laid out temptingly on a table on the wide veranda.

William handled crowd control on the sidewalk along with a young officer appointed by Mac. As the party-goers chatted amiably in the near-dark of the party, waiting for their tours, the night sky began to cloud over and lightning flashed.

"They can't all stand out here with that storm coming up," the young police officer worried, turning up her collar against the wind that started to bluster through the surrounding trees.

William agreed. "They'll have to stuff themselves inside, but we'll manage. You're just in time, Clive," William said, seeing that Clive had finished handing out all the numbers. "Take as many as possible to the enclosed veranda off the dining room. There is plenty of food for them to indulge." He slapped his friend's back lightly.

Everyone could be heard exclaiming over the approaching thunder. The storm picked up momentum quickly. Winds whipped around the Queen Anne mansion and the dimmed lights flickered off and on. Mac left Bryce for a few minutes and hurried to the main breaker box to make sure the storm didn't put them into complete darkness. He feared that the storm would bring even more trouble on top of the troubling vandalism of the upstairs room.

The breaker box looked fine, but Mac could hear the rumbles of thunder begin to pour through the town and echo off the harbor and the sea. Sweetfern Harbor was in for a frightful storm, he thought, and headed back to the party.

CHAPTER FOUR

"**L**isten to those winds," Allie said, watching the autumn trees swaying dangerously against the stormy sky. Hope and David Williams stood next to their daughter in the foyer while the third tour group formed behind her. "This is a perfect night for a ghost tour." She shivered with anticipation.

"I'm glad there are lanterns," Hope said. "This storm could put us in complete darkness."

"This is a real Fright Night," Molly said. The Morning Sun Coffee owner nudged closer to Jon Wright, the boat rental shop owner, who looked pleased to have Molly by his side. They were dressed as a pair of tattered skeletons. "I can't wait to walk through this place on a night like this."

Molly and Jon joined her mother's group. Phyllis

switched on her lantern and primly cleared her throat. Anyone who thought that perhaps the older woman would be less of an interesting tour guide found themselves proved wrong when Phyllis assumed a spooky, dramatic voice and whispered to the group, her eyes glittering in the dark. "Well, are you prepared to be scared? Follow me...if you dare..." Phyllis gave a merry cackle and swept her witch's cloak behind her as the delighted tour group followed her.

Brenda talked in a low voice to her group at the top of the stairway. Each carried a lantern and listened intently as she began telling ghost stories. This was perhaps Brenda's favorite part. There had been far too many true tragedies that had visited Sheffield Bed and Breakfast, but Fright Night was her chance to make up stories that were not sad but filled instead with drama and excitement. "A disillusioned young woman met her death on this very step," Brenda intoned, glancing down at the stairs with a tragic expression, "when she collapsed and died. The tale is told that she died of fright...because she knew the house's secrets...and the house knew hers..."

A few guests stumbled at her final words. Brenda smiled to herself and admired her ability to weave scary stories. To her knowledge, nothing paranormal had ever happened at Sheffield Bed and Breakfast, either before or after Randolph Sheffield restored it. However, the guests didn't need to know that.

Brenda slowed her pace and waved her lantern gently over her head and cautioned everyone. "Beware...here lurk the shadows only few have seen. You may meet, when the veil is thin, figures and creatures from other dimensions." She had enlisted the porter Michael to play the part of such a creature, and true to form, his acting abilities put the fear of Halloween into the guests as he loomed out from behind a hidden closet door, startling them all in his pale makeup and tattered clothes. Heading down the passage, they dodged hideous puppets that swung in their faces as Brenda led them down a narrow passageway before arriving at the bottom of the twisting, constricted staircase that led up to the tower. She turned and faced them all. Lightning flashed just before she spoke. Silently, she jumped for joy at this dramatic moment, although she kept her face carefully sad and dramatic.

"These stairs are very narrow. No one can possibly turn and go back until you reach the top. There is a spell that was cast centuries ago on this land: once a journey starts, one cannot turn back until it is completed." She waved her lantern gently again while thunder crashed outside. Wind whistled louder along the rooftop and through the trees outside as they made their way higher in the building.

Phyllis followed Brenda a few minutes later with her group. Phyllis and Allie came up with new stories of their own. Phyllis was ready and was an excellent actress as she led the ghost tour. When one of her tourists asked if they would find secret rooms, Phyllis said possibly, but to be careful. "I have worked here for many, many years, and I know the sad truth...once a hidden door has been opened, you cannot close it again. The person who opens it may never be seen again, in fact." She took her time, walking along the planked hallway in silence. She suddenly stopped and held up her lantern.

She asked her group to listen carefully. "There she is!" Phyllis moaned. "The lonely crying of the woman hidden in the walls!" She was pleased when the thunder crashed again, and rain pummeled down. The whistling wind sounded eerily like a woman crying at times, so that even Phyllis shivered a little to hear it. Several in the group screamed at the sound. Phyllis motioned for them to continue. When she saw Brenda leading her group down the back stairs from the attic, she knew it was her turn to lead her group up to the tower.

When Brenda returned to the foyer, she laughed with Hope and David after bidding her tour group farewell. "They believed every word. When you take over for Allie later, make sure you have some good stories to tell. The spookier, the better."

"We're ready," David said. He explained he had sound effects to accompany them, recorded on his phone from the TV station where he was an anchor.

By the time Brenda escorted her third tour group, the

storm had subsided somewhat, though the wind continued to whip around the building. When she led the people near her old apartment at the end of the hall, she stopped. Her group held their breath and waited. Brenda leaned against the wall and listened.

Guests took her actions as part of the entertainment, but Brenda was sure she heard something scratching. Her act fell away as she listened intently, attempting to ferret out the source of the sound. Perhaps it was simply drips in the drainpipes from the rain, she told herself. She finally shook her head and stepped away. Brenda made a mental note to call an emergency exterminator the next day. One of the tourists asked what was behind the wall, smiling big and waiting for a good story.

"It could be anything," she said in a matter-of-fact tone, contemplating what Chef Pierre had said before and making a disgusted face, thinking of rats. Suddenly, she remembered what she was supposed to be doing and her voice returned to a conspiratorial tone. "No one knows. The walls have ears! The walls know secrets. Stand back in case something comes right through that wall to steal your thoughts from you." Everyone moved to the center of the passageway, delighted with her tales.

Brenda hesitated once more and then moved on with her group. She employed a reliable exterminator to come every year and make sure no animals nested in the basement or found their way into the building. Her chefs always diligently checked the food storage areas for signs of rodents, and none had been seen in years. The exterminator always checked the roof and basement and any other place an animal could possibly burrow its way in. Chef Pierre had been right about hearing scratching, Brenda thought with dismay. Whatever it was had found its way all the way to the second floor and probably higher. She hoped it was something nice, like perhaps a bird's nest that would be easy to remove and not something nasty like a diseased rodent.

Karina and Grace were in the group following behind her and traded conspiracy theories. "There must be a secret room after all," Grace said.

Karina poked her and said maybe it was a squirrel. "It's an old building, Karina. And it could be the storm outside, too. Maybe branches are brushing against the outside."

Brenda knew it was time to get her group back on track with the eerie stories they had come for. She resumed her tales and sensed the fear and delight returning in the tourists.

When they returned to the foyer, William asked Brenda if she wanted a break and he would fill in for her. "You look a bit tense, Brenda. Is everything all right?"

"I'm fine, just thinking about maintenance issues. It's an old house, our work is never done, I guess. I am a bit tired, though…perhaps I'll do one more and then perhaps you or someone else could take over, William. Phyllis is probably ready for a break, too."

Brenda began her fourth tour. When they got to the spot where she heard scratching, she stopped again, trying to make it part of her act to listen at the wall, but she dropped the story she was telling because she heard a distinct sound. Brenda was certain this time someone coughed from behind the wall. Three tourists near Brenda swore they heard the same thing. Their lanterns swung a little from shaking hands.

"Is the creature in that wall, Brenda?" a young woman asked. "Tell us the story. It is a story, right? Not something real?"

Brenda looked at her and said, "Perhaps it is real, we'll never know…we will never know since there is no doorway or room behind this wall that could allow a real person to be there. Be careful. Old houses hold secrets. That is my only advice for now." She tried to make it sound like part of the story, but in truth, she worried more and more.

"Remember, it is Halloween," one man jested. "We should expect something like this. It's all a prop, isn't it, Brenda? You've got something in there rigged to twitch around and make a sound in a hidden panel or something, right?"

Brenda's thoughts were interrupted by his remark. She knew she had a skeptic in the group. She produced an eerie smile in the lantern light and said she had no tricks up her sleeves. "It was probably spirits from long ago," she said. She used her low growling voice in answer. "The ghosts of people who were here centuries ago, no doubt."

Brenda hoped she scared the tourists as they expected, though the rest of the tour was a blur and she scarcely remembered getting through it. She found Mac when she was done and asked him to come to the kitchen with her. William took her place in the tours and he and Phyllis combined the final tours together. Hope and David finished up for Allie.

Brenda and Mac sat alone in the kitchen, Brenda drinking a cup of hot chamomile tea. Chef Pierre and his helpers had finished the kitchen work and were all sitting on the screened-in back porch off the kitchen to watch the final fury of the storm.

"I heard scratching during one of the tours," Brenda told Mac. "It came from the wall toward the end of the second-floor hallway. I was sure a small animal was in there until a couple of tours later, I swear I heard someone cough from behind the wall."

Mac stared at her. "You are just tired, Brenda. You're getting too deep into the storytelling of the night. This has been quite a party, and we still haven't concluded how someone managed to get into the Meyers' room and ransack it."

"There is no way I'm tired at this point, Mac. I'm wired, but not tired." She smiled weakly and took another sip of tea. "I know I heard something in that wall. There is no doorway behind it, and no room there, either. But I know I heard scratching and then a cough."

Mac reached for her hand. "It was in the middle of a severe storm, Brenda. It was probably caused by that. Or it came from somewhere else. You said it yourself—there's no room there, so how could anyone get behind that wall?"

Brenda shook her head. "I don't know, but I know I heard what I heard."

"Did anyone else hear it?"

"A couple of people near me heard the cough."

"I really think all of you heard storm sounds, but we can explore in the morning to make sure." He chuckled. "That must have added suspense to your already spooky tour." Brenda didn't find humor in that moment but tried to keep her head.

"Let's stay over here in our old apartment tonight," Brenda said. "We both have to get up extra early tomorrow, and I'll have a day of clean-up. We also must find out who broke into the Meyers' room. We can't let that slide just because nothing was taken." Mac agreed. "There is sure to be a reasonable explanation," she said, "but what?"

Lauren and Ryan joined in with others during the party. Neither opted to take a tour. They felt they had had enough excitement and hoped the detectives could get to the bottom of their situation before they settled in for the night. Detective Rivers checked in with them one last time before everyone retired. He told the Meyers couple that the investigation was in the beginning stages, but they would get to the bottom of it all.

"Keep your door locked and call right away if you need us. Brenda and I will be down the hall tonight in her former apartment. We checked the lock on your door, and it appears to be secure."

The reality of the situation was that no unknown fingerprints were detected in the room or on the door latch into the room. Privately, Mac considered the possibility the young couple purposely set it all up to go along with the Halloween mood of the bed and breakfast. And yet, that didn't prevent him from performing an official security audit of the entire event. Besides, he reasoned, they appeared genuinely scared and upset.

After Ryan locked the door for the night, Lauren remained tense. "I don't think Detective Rivers believes someone came in here and threw our things around. I know I had nothing to do with it, and we were together the whole time, but he doesn't believe us."

"Let's get some sleep, Lauren," Ryan said, removing some of his zombie makeup with a washcloth. "I'm sure Mac is simply following protocol. As he told us, they are in the beginning stages. There's a lot more for them to look in to. Besides, it is after midnight, and we need to get some sleep. I think I'll sleep in tomorrow morning." Brenda had informed her guests that breakfast would begin an hour later than usual. He flopped down on the pillow, then rolled over and hugged his wife. "That's not to say that if you wake up early, I'd say no to you bringing me breakfast in bed."

"I think I'd have to be fully awake to consider that." They laughed, and Lauren gave her husband her last words of the night. "I love you more than anything in this world, Ryan. After a late sleep-in and breakfast in bed, we should talk. I think there is something I should tell you about. But it can wait for tomorrow morning."

Ryan attempted to force her to tell him right away. "Is it something about the ransacking of our room? I can't believe you are going to torture me until morning. Tell me now."

"It's a long story, and we're already bushed." Lauren didn't want him to bolt in the middle of the night once he learned what happened when she was a young girl.

Ryan pulled her closer and told her he expected to hear her story over morning coffee. "I suppose I have no choice since you seem bent on waiting to tell me. Nothing you tell me could possibly mar my feelings for you, Lauren. I hope you know that."

She relaxed and snuggled closer. Both fell asleep right away.

In the quiet of the bed and breakfast, the Meyerses missed hearing the soft click of the door opening.

Lauren found herself startling awake in silence without knowing why. Then she felt the sinister presence of the intruder. She didn't move, frozen in place as she waited for the person to once again ransack their room while he thought they slept. She wanted to awaken Ryan, but feared that any movement might cause the person to get violent. Beneath the covers, she tried to make out the size of the person. She was sure it was a man, but other than that, she had no clue regarding his features.

Without warning, the figure moved abruptly towards the bed. A knife slipped quickly from the man's pocket and he thrust it into Ryan's chest and again into his neck.

A splash of blood hit Lauren's face in the dark. The last garbled sound that escaped her husband's lips would remain in her memory for a long time. As the figure left the room as fast as he had arrived, Lauren gasped when she at last thought she recognized him. She felt the warm trickle of fluid that escaped Ryan's lifeless body and onto hers. Reality struck, and her blood-curdling scream echoed throughout the corridors of the bed and breakfast.

Brenda sat up in bed. Mac heard the noise too, and both rushed to the hallway. Several guests stuck their heads out from their rooms in sleepy concern and confusion. Detective Rivers motioned for them to go back into their rooms. Brenda rushed along behind him.

"I have no idea what is going on," Marcus told Jolene as he closed the door, "but we should lock the door in case this is the real thing and not a Halloween prank."

"That didn't sound like a prank," Jolene said. "I think something terrible has happened. It sounded like it came from the Meyers' room. I heard their room was ransacked earlier today."

Marcus had not heard that, and his wife told him of the rumors floating around during the party about the incident. Jolene shivered. "I was nearby one tour when Brenda stopped and listened for something she heard through one of the walls on this floor. I don't know what that was all about, but it didn't look like it was part of the fun storytelling. She said the storm sent strange sounds through the bed and breakfast, but behind her mask I saw fear. Or perhaps it was uncertainty in her eyes. Those lantern lights cast eerie shadows, especially along that passageway near the tower stairs."

"Calm down, Jolene. We'll find out soon enough if anything is amiss. Let's just lay low until the morning. We need to get our sleep. I'm sure whatever she heard was due to the severe storms going on...perhaps someone had a nightmare." Marcus checked the door again and was assured it was locked.

Brenda walked quickly around Mac to meet Lauren Meyers as she opened the door and started to run out. Brenda caught her in her arms and told her to tell them what happened. It was then that Mac saw the sure signs of fresh blood staining the right side of her nightclothes.

Lauren's hands shook violently as she pointed into their room. "Ryan. He's...on the bed. He's not moving. Someone...did something very bad to him."

Mac noted that her words in a state of shock resembled one a child would relate. He hurried inside the room and flipped on the overhead light. The bed was saturated with red. The gruesome spectacle that was Ryan Meyers' body came as a shock even to the detective. The attack had been a brutal one. He immediately called for backup and specifically asked the dispatcher to send Officer Natalie Sims along with the others. He knew that Lauren Meyers would need her.

"Is something really going on, or is this just a late Halloween prank?" Grace Mitchell padded down the hallway toward Brenda and the distraught Lauren.

"Not a prank. Something has happened, Grace," Brenda said. "I want everyone to go back to their rooms and stay there. Lock your doors and wait until we can talk with each of you."

All guests who ventured again from their rooms readily obeyed her orders, looking somewhat shocked. They all realized no Halloween prank was involved and sobered at the thought.

"It's not good, Karina," Grace said with worry weighing down her voice. She closed the door of their room behind her and quickly locked it. "I think something awful has happened. Everything seems to be coming from the area of the Meyers' room."

Karina shivered. "Are you sure it isn't more of Fright Night?"

"I'm sure. I heard Mac talk to someone on the phone and ask for backup. If a crime has been committed, we must be careful. Whoever committed it may very well still be in the building."

"I wish we could see what is going on," Karina said. "That scream was horrible. I guess something really did happen." She crept to the door and checked the latch again. "Let's just stay low for now. With police around, I think we're as safe as we can be."

"I agree, Karina. Whoever did something likely didn't stick around anyway. I think he is long gone by now."

Officer Sims arrived not long after and hurried down the hallway to the scene of the crime. Brenda told her Lauren needed to change into clean clothing since her pajamas would be evidence. "I'll get sweats for her from her closet and she can change downstairs." She drew Natalie aside. "Make sure you take photos of every part of her body, especially her hands. Bag her clothing, please. We need any DNA we can get. I'll meet you both in the sitting room in about fifteen minutes." They retrieved clothing for Lauren, and Natalie escorted the shaken woman down the staircase to change and take care of the evidence photography.

Brenda rejoined her husband. She was shocked at the scene to see the body that appeared ripped apart on the bed. "This was a brutal one, Brenda," Mac said. "So far, I doubt we'll find new fingerprints, but it will be a while before we're through in here. The coroner is on his way."

Brenda told Mac of her instructions to Officer Sims. "It is early enough that signs of a struggle or similar actions will be visible on Lauren." Brenda and Mac focused on examining the room for any additional clues, not convinced they would find much.

Downstairs in the office, once Lauren was in clean clothing again, Officer Sims began to gently prod her on events that had taken place. She had not asked about her husband yet. It was something Officer Sims made a mental note of. She decided to be blunt.

"How did you know Ryan was dead?"

A blank stare crossed Lauren's face. A few seconds later, she answered. "I saw it happen. I know who did this. He meant to kill me, not Ryan."

"How do you know this?"

"It's been years, but I've never forgotten that man."

Officer Sims offered her hot tea from the beverage nook and she accepted. The officer went to fetch the tea and reflected on this new development. Natalie knew the woman's answers were something she should wait for Brenda to delve into, but her instructions had been to get information. If Lauren Meyers was willing to talk, then Natalie decided to go forward with it.

"Is this other man a guest here?"

Lauren's short laugh was sharp. "The only place he's been a guest is a mental hospital. Ever since I was fourteen. I'm twenty-six now. Twelve years may seem like a long time, but no amount of years will be long enough for him."

Officer Sims breathed a deep sigh of relief when she saw Brenda enter the sitting room. She met her, and they stood in the doorway. They talked in low tones while shooting glances at Lauren. She twisted her fingers and then wiped the moisture that accumulated onto her sweatpants. Officer Sims related the conversation.

"Of course, she is in shock. I haven't gotten much from her other than what I've told you."

Brenda asked Natalie to remain in the room. She sat down across from Lauren.

"Officer Sims tells me you told her that whoever did this is in a mental institution. How do you know he was the one in your room? Are you sure?" Lauren nodded vigorously. "How could he have gotten out of a hospital?"

In short gasps, Lauren insisted he must have escaped. She began to sob. "I know it was him. I know it was. It was dark, but I saw him."

Brenda wasn't so sure. "How did you recognize him?"

Lauren bent her head, hiding her tears behind one hand. "I just knew. I saw the form and not the face of the person, but I knew. No one forgets the shape of a murderer."

CHAPTER FIVE

Brenda didn't know what to think. Above all, who was the mysterious man Lauren alluded to? No amount of prying produced a name, due to Lauren's shock or grief or some combination of fear and confusion. Brenda spent an hour with the wife of the murdered victim. Much of that time was spent listening to the sobs that didn't stop. Brenda asked her once again who she thought killed her husband.

"I am terrified. You must understand why I can't give you his name. He'll come back for me and succeed next time." Lauren buried her head into her hands and shook her head. When she sat up straight, her face was pale as a china doll's. "He's hated me for a long time. I saw what he did once and now he is back. He should be in a prison with guards to make sure he doesn't escape. He got away.

And now, I've lost Ryan because of him." Sobs racked her body.

When Brenda worriedly suggested that perhaps Lauren needed to go to a hospital to take some medication to calm down, Lauren sat bolt upright and looked terrified. "No. He could be there waiting for me." After a while longer, she calmed down, at least enough to provide a few more details. "It was horrible. He kept stabbing and stabbing. He's a madman but he knew what he was doing."

"Try to take deep breaths, Lauren. We can get moving faster if we know who we are looking for."

It was as if Lauren didn't hear her words. Her mind was pummeled with the swift actions of the man who killed the love of her life. Seth Hill's mother swiped Seth from her, and now the intruder did the same by taking Ryan's life. She had nothing left to live for. She felt Brenda's hand on her hand.

"I'm never going to be safe again," Lauren said. "He will always manage to find me until he finally takes me, too."

Lauren sank back onto the sofa and closed her eyes. She wished she had told Ryan about her fears. She wished she had told him the whole story before they went to bed, just as he had begged her. He would have done something to bar the door, so they could get a restful sleep. Now she would never bring him breakfast in bed, never see his handsome face sleeping, never feel his love again. She would only see his form, gasping and sputtering, bloody in the darkness under the knife of a murderer.

Lauren had considered telling Ryan everything before they were married. She lost courage, and then decided after six months of marriage she would wait to know him better and learn more about how he might react. Those months passed and turned into years and she still held back, reluctant to break the spell. Perhaps, she often reasoned, if she ignored it, the entire thing would go away. But how wrong she had been. The facts hounded her mind and made tears streak down her face anew.

"If I had only told Ryan everything, he would still have loved me, don't you think so, Brenda? He would have kept me safe. He would."

Brenda assured her that Ryan seemed like an understanding man. However, Lauren would not explain what she thought threatened her husband's love for her. Brenda again tried to convince Lauren to tell her the story she failed to relate to Ryan. Her only response was how afraid she was.

It was three in the morning, and officers had been assigned to every outside entry into Sheffield Bed and Breakfast. Brenda failed to get more information from the distraught Lauren Meyers. Officer Sims was joined by Officer Swenson and they sat with Lauren. They were aware the killer remained on the loose. Natalie offered the woman another cup of hot tea while they waited.

"I just want to sleep and forget it all," Lauren said. She left the paisley chair and sat on the edge of the sofa.

"I'm sure if you want to rest, it will be fine."

Almost at once, Lauren laid down and fell into a deep sleep. Natalie took the opportunity to take note of her skin. There were no abrasions or indications of any kind that led Natalie to believe Lauren had experienced any kind of a struggle. The only evidence of possible involvement were Ryan's blood stains on one side of her gown, which was now bagged and labeled carefully as evidence.

Upstairs, Brenda stood next to her husband until the coroner finished his job at the bedside. "Multiple stab wounds to strategic places on the body. His death was quick." He motioned for his assistants to move the body to the stretcher and carry it to the van so it could be taken to the morgue.

"I'm not sure how," Mac said, "but it could be his wife who committed this crime. I think she threw things around in here earlier without Ryan knowing it and then pretended it was an intruder. She is the only possible one right now."

Brenda wasn't so sure, but she understood why her husband considered the possibility. No one else had entered the room, according to lack of evidence so far, and the dead person's spouse was almost always the first suspect to be evaluated. She recalled Officer Sims's conversation.

Brenda shook her head slowly. "It may be misdirection, but Lauren told Natalie she knows who did it." Brenda told Mac about the interview in the sitting room. "I can't figure out how anyone could have gained access to a guest room. I suppose we should find out everything we can from the hospital about a possible escapee. Lauren did mention the name of the hospital. It's Rocky Mountain Medical Institution, located a few miles from Denver."

"She could be pinning it on someone like that, but those mental hospitals take precautions. Did she give an explanation for how someone could have escaped without being missed?"

"No, she didn't. She clammed up and wouldn't tell me anything else. Natalie didn't get anything from her either."

"We should think about how someone could even get in the building without being seen. We know the building was locked up tight at night. Perhaps with the crowds here during the celebration someone could have possibly slipped in and hidden in the building. But how did anyone get in during the time earlier when the room was ransacked?"

"That wouldn't have been that hard. Allie had left and the rest of us were at dinner. It's true the main door in front was locked during that time. Pierre didn't see anyone unusual come through the back door, but he and his helpers were busy with dinner, too. It is possible someone slipped up the back stairs."

Mac had to agree with her points. He knew the best person on the force to handle research and discover the impossible was his son-in-law, who he allowed to be off during the nightshifts until his and Jenny's baby arrived. Bryce had left to check on his wife. Detective Bryce Jones could do his research work from home. Mac called him and updated him on events. Bryce was anxious to start working. He missed working cases in the middle of the night, but he loved Jenny so much that the thought of leaving her alone now didn't enter his mind. He retrieved his laptop and began the investigation into a possible escapee from the mental hospital in Colorado. He would make phone calls from his nook at the end of the hall where he could hear Jenny and work at the same time.

When Mac ended his call to Bryce, Brenda told him she was going to explore the hallway and find out what was behind the walls. "We can interview all the guests right after breakfast. I'm sure they've gone back to bed by now." She felt for the small flashlight in the pocket of her sweats.

Mac produced a half grin. "You can believe someone is

behind those walls if you wish, Brenda, but I don't think you'll find anything more than a few squirrels." When he saw the defiance in his wife's eyes, he relented. "Maybe you did hear a person, but the question is, how could anyone actually hide behind walls that have no entries?" The detective also considered that if his wife was correct, the person would be long gone by now. He shook his head to clear thoughts of the impossible scenario.

Brenda ignored him. She found the secluded end of the hallway where she had heard sounds during her tours and tapped along the wall. Reality told her she rapped on a solid wall, but there was also the fact she heard not only scratching, but a distinct cough. Deep into her thoughts, she kept pressing and rapping along the wall, listening for sounds. Suddenly, she jerked back when the solid wall gave way. She pushed gently, and it slid open with the soft sound of a creaking hinge on the other side. Her heart beat faster. She considered going back for assistance until she realized if the murderer had been someone hiding out behind walls, he surely had escaped by now. No criminal hangs around a gruesome murder scene like this one, she thought.

She stepped into the musty, dark space behind the panel that opened, trying to figure out how big it was. She stumbled forward when she didn't encounter a wall and was startled when the door suddenly snapped closed behind her. Her thumb felt for the switch and her flashlight beamed a soft light. Brenda was thrilled and shocked that she didn't know of this hidden, narrow passageway. If she had, it certainly would have been featured on the Halloween tour.

There was just enough room for one person to walk through the narrow space at a time. It seemed to lead between two walls, and she realized she was moving parallel to the main second-floor corridor, toward the rear of the building. There must be a concealed, narrow stairway leading down just ahead, though she couldn't see it yet.

Her mind racing, she started guessing where else this passage might possibly lead, and then she had a flash of insight. The stone seawall that bordered the beach along the Sheffield House property climbed up the lawns all the way to the back corner of the building, where it transitioned into a charming part of the rock-bordered garden. The gardens were tidy and well-known to her groundskeepers, but there were several places in the larger wall itself where the stones were too large to be moved—surely the passageway must come out somewhere among those tumble-down stones. There were several places where the stones were easily tall enough to hide a door or a narrow entryway, she guessed.

A dank odor laced with faint humidity hit her face. Brenda sniffed briefly and picked up a stale cigarette scent. Brenda walked along slowly while she cursed herself for not figuring out the existence of the passageway earlier. She hoped to find the stairwell and then pick up the scent of soothing salt air at any moment. It was only a matter of time before she would finally find the outlet.

The bent figure leapt in front of her as if he emerged from the dank stone wall itself. Brenda dropped her flashlight in shock, and it spun wildly, coming to a rest on the floor. The beam was now pointed only indirectly at the man, who she tried to look in the eye. "Hello?" Her heart raced. He did not answer her. His eyes were dark and wild-looking. He shifted back and forth in a nervous feinting movement. The thought was ludicrous, but he did remind her of a stray cat that used to shuffle in a similar way on the fence in her backyard during her childhood in Michigan.

A growl and then a suppressed cough escaped the figure's mouth. It matched what she heard during the tour. Thoughts of her own safety raced through her mind. Only Mac knew she had gone to explore, but he had no idea that the wall opened into a passageway. She was on her own with the menacing creature in front of her.

Brenda's hostess mode took over and she worried about the bedraggled, ill-looking man in front of her. "May I help you in some way?" She tried not to shudder when she saw the knife handle partially sticking out from his pocket in the dim gloom.

Her question was answered with a sneer. His teeth bared,

and she noticed his clenched fists. A fleeting observation of something dark on his knuckles disturbed her—blood? Or something more innocent, like mud? She stored it away for later.

"You think I owe you something? Ha. You wouldn't be the first person to invade my privacy. I kill anyone who tries," he said. His tone snarled.

"I apologize for intruding," she said. Brenda nervously glanced down at the flashlight, wondering if it was heavy enough to act as a weapon, if she could grab it.

"Leave the flashlight," he sneered. "I've been in here for days and even on a bright day I can see like a cat in the dark, so don't think you can make any clever moves."

Moisture slicked her palms. "I'll leave you alone and won't bother you again." She didn't want to turn her back on him. His demeanor sent the message that he wasn't going to relent. Not giving up completely, she asked him another question as she shuffled backward carefully. "Where does this hallway end? I was hoping to get a whiff of the ocean air soon."

His facial expression told her his anger was increasing the longer she stuck around. She turned to go and jerked backward when he burst forward and grasped his strong hand on her shoulder. His clutch clenched tightly enough to cause bruising and she gasped in pain.

"You can stay here as long as you want to. I won't tell anyone you are here," Brenda tried to bargain.

"That depends on who you are," his voice rasped. "I heard those crazy people last night call someone Brenda. Is that you?" She nodded frantically. "Then you must be someone important. In that case, I'm not so sure I can let you off that easily."

Brenda had to quickly decide on her response. If he knew she owned the bed and breakfast, would that reassure him she was sincere when giving permission for him to stay behind the wall? She had to chance it.

"I own this building. I never knew there was a hidden hallway. I was just exploring in case some of the guests wanted to see hidden spaces like this. I didn't mean to disturb you—"

"It's hard to believe that you were exploring after midnight. I would think you'd be sleeping."

"There was an accident in one of the rooms! I was up anyway!"

A chuckle mixed in with his sneer. He pushed her along the narrow corridor ahead of him now, until she guessed they were a few yards from the panel that she knew could set her free. It was now pitch black, and her flashlight was behind them, shedding no light on this area now. "I don't trust you. You seem like a nice lady, but I'll be long gone by the time you find your way back." He roughly shoved her forward and disappeared into the pitch black, leaving her standing in the stone passage in the pitch dark.

Brenda failed to calculate how far she had walked through the narrow hall. At first, disorientation set in and she fumbled along the irregular limestone wall. She took deep breaths. The dark passage grew quiet. Faint cigarette odor lingered. She had no idea if he lurked a few feet from her or if he had slipped out of the building entirely. Then she heard his voice some distance away, menacing and unstable.

"Go on. Get out of here. If you take much longer, I may change my mind about letting you go. And no one would find you in here for days, I'm sure..."

Brenda didn't respond, simply continued walking and tried to suppress the fear that fluttered in her stomach. She continued to feel her way along the pitch-black passageway. No more words came from the man's mouth. She tried to concentrate on his location but panicked and focused on finding a way out, and soon. Muffled sounds reached her. They came from the second floor. She heard faint footsteps on the floor above her. Guests were moving around. She wondered if she dared to call out for help, or if the man would rush forward and stab her for such a thing.

She hoped the guests were preparing to return to bed until she recalled daylight neared. She knew rumors would fly not only throughout Sheffield Bed and

Breakfast, but also run rampant through Sweetfern Harbor by morning time. Brenda couldn't allow herself to think about the reputation of her bed and breakfast at this point. She had to get out of the dank hallway.

She finally felt a smoother surface and discovered a narrow metal latch. When she pulled on it, hallway light from the second floor almost blinded her and she stumbled out into the open once again. Brenda almost sobbed with relief.

She heard Mac's voice along with other officers. The door closed behind her and it became the smooth wall that lined the second floor once again. She leaned against it and took deep breaths.

"Brenda, Lauren Meyers wants to talk with you," one of the officers called up, having no idea what she had just been through.

"I'll be down as soon as possible." She attempted to still her overactive heartbeat.

She hurried to Mac and told him of her experience. Then she showed him how to open the wall. The detective summoned two officers to follow him into the passageway.

"He still has the knife in his pocket. Be careful," Brenda said. "There are droplets of blood on the floor."

"We'll get to the bottom of this, Brenda. Find out all you

can from Lauren, and I'll meet you later downstairs. Are you up to it?" Mac asked. "Are you okay? Did he hurt you?" His face was filled with concern as he searched his beloved wife for any damage, but Brenda was tougher than she seemed.

She reassured him with a quick hug. "I have to keep going. He didn't touch me, not really. Just a bruise on my shoulder, I think. My adrenaline is still at its peak. I may crash later when I realize how close I came to becoming another of his victims. I am sure he killed Ryan Meyers. I saw what I believe were blood stains on his knuckles, too."

"We'll find him." The detective was assured his wife was all right for now and took off down the passage with his officers.

Brenda knew that Lauren Meyers could tell her plenty. She was anxious to talk with her. When she entered the sitting room, she saw a tear-streaked face. Officer Sims told Brenda at the doorway that Lauren was still in shock from the impact of what had happened to her husband.

"I don't think she had anything to do with it all," Natalie said. "She is shaken up considerably. I think she will need a sedative."

"I'll offer again to go to the hospital. Maybe she'll tell me what she knows. Why don't you take a break for a while, Natalie? I'll stay with her until Mac gets down here."

Lauren sat on the edge of the sofa and waited tensely for Brenda to enter the room.

"Lauren, I know you have had a horrible night of it. I understand you wanted to talk with me again." She pulled a portable recorder from her pocket. "I'd like to record your words."

Lauren nodded her head vigorously. "I'm ready now. What I will tell you is the truth. I want to tell you the story I promised Ryan I would tell him before he—before it happened." She swallowed nervously but persevered. "Now he will never know of my deception." She sniffled loudly, and Brenda handed her a tissue. "I deceived him because if I had told him the truth before we married, he would have left me like Seth Hill did. I loved Seth, but when his mother snooped around and discovered my background, she forbade him to marry me. We were in love. I didn't think I'd ever love again until I met Ryan." She reached for another tissue. "I was afraid to tell him what happened in my past for fear of losing him, too."

"Why don't you start from the beginning?"

CHAPTER SIX

L auren Meyers took a deep breath and began telling her story to Brenda. At last, she could tell everything in full. Perhaps, now that she had lost almost everything dear to her, the telling would finally free her.

"My mother was killed in a car accident a couple of years before I became a teenager. My father, Grady, began drinking heavily and chose to ignore me. He had no idea who my friends were, and I didn't dare invite them to our house. I couldn't rely on him being sober. When I turned fourteen, my aunt and uncle invited me to their home to celebrate. It was the best birthday I had had since my mother's death. My friends came, and we even had a local band perform. They were unknown to me at the time, but they played our kind of music."

"Did your father approve of the party?"

WENDY MEADOWS

"I don't think he even knew about it. My aunt and uncle certainly didn't invite him. Besides, he was too busy brawling with our neighbor. The elderly man who lived next door, his name was Randy...I don't recall his last name right now. I thought he was a nice person, but my dad sure didn't. Well, after that birthday party, I got home and discovered him even more drunk than ever. He was berating Randy for planting a stupid tree on our property. Randy said he had proof it was on his property, but that didn't matter to my father. He was on a rampage by that time. He called it an invasion of his privacy."

Brenda shivered when Lauren said those words.

"I was standing at my upstairs bedroom window watching his latest tirade against that poor innocent man next door. I knew my father was as drunk as I'd ever seen him. I was just thinking I should call my aunt and ask to stay with them for the whole night—and maybe for the rest of my high school years, because I had had so much fun at the party and had started to remember what it was like not to live in fear all the time. And then...it happened. I saw my father pull out a long knife and plunge it into Randy's chest." Lauren shuddered as if seeing it for the first time. "That one stab wasn't enough. He did it over and over. I later heard the poor man had thirty-six stab wounds."

"That's terrible. I'm so sorry you saw that as such a young girl. What did you do?"

"I didn't want my father to know I had been watching and so I quickly pulled away from the window and turned my music up higher. The old man's daughter drove up just after my father got out of sight. I heard the wailing when she discovered the bloody body of her father."

Lauren sank lower into the folds of the sofa. She curled up as if to protect herself from the memories. Brenda waited. The recorder ran silently, recording the woman's long pause as she considered her next words. "I'll never forget that night. It changed me. It's why I lost Seth..."

"I don't understand how your boyfriend Seth came into it. It's not as if you played a part in any of it," Brenda said. "Did your father know you saw him do it? Did he spread around stories or something?"

She shook her head no. "He had no idea I witnessed anything until I turned him in. When the police started canvassing the neighborhood, they naturally came to our house first. We lived right next door. I knew if my father could be as vicious as that, it wouldn't take much to set him off against me. I felt awful, but I had to turn in my own father just to stay safe. I ended up staying with my aunt and uncle...but not for the reasons I thought. I had to stay with them so I wouldn't become a ward of the state."

"Where was your father when the police talked with you?"

"He was in the backseat of the police car by then. He had to give them permission to talk with me alone. He had no idea I was a witness to the whole thing. He was always yelling at me to turn down my music. I guess he thought I was listening to music or something and hadn't heard or seen anything. Well, I told the police the truth, and Grady Fisher was booked for murder. Later, I found out they had plenty of evidence against him from the bloody clothes my father had simply left in our garage and the knife that still dripped with the man's blood. He was so drunk he had simply dropped the knife on the kitchen floor and left it there until the next morning when the police showed up."

"How did he end up in a mental hospital and not prison?"

Lauren gave a short, bitter laugh. "From the moment they arrested him, he began to put on the crazy act. I mean, he must have been an awful person to get so drunk and then to do something so horrible, but I never thought he was insane. I thought he was a mean man who drank too much." Circles began to form under her eyes. "I am sure he was here, in this bed and breakfast. I know I recognized him when he left the room after killing Ryan. Those same sloping shoulders...that same gait...and I know he thought I was on that side of the bed and he meant to kill me. That night Ryan fell asleep first on my side and then I took his side."

"How would your father have known which side you typically slept on?"

Lauren stopped to think about this for a moment. "I haven't been able to put this into words before now, but I believe my father escaped the hospital some time ago and found his way here. He must have kept track of me all these years and somehow knew I'd be here this weekend. Perhaps he picked it knowing about the secret passage allowing him access to the house. I feel sure he wanted to punish me, to frame me for my own husband's death, as a punishment for turning my own father in to the police. But once his handwriting is proven, you will all believe me that it was him." She paused and looked up at Brenda. "Maybe he has been watching us at night to know which side I slept on." She shuddered again and wrapped her arms around her body.

Brenda asked her how handwriting entered the picture. Lauren reached into her pocket and pulled out a crumpled piece of paper, revealing the note she found the day the room was ransacked. She confessed she had crumpled the note and dropped it, wanting to conceal it from her husband, and had later found it somewhere on the floor near the window in the room. Brenda took out her cell and notified Mac of the further evidence. Her attention then reverted to her guest.

"He's still here, Brenda," Lauren said. "He knew it wasn't

a woman he killed. He is just waiting to get the right victim, and that is me."

Brenda was now certain Grady Fisher was in the building, or at least he had been. She recalled the conversation she had with him. He had answered coherently, though cruelly. She realized there were no signs he was a madman from the way his words connected with her subject matter.

"You will have twenty-four-hour protection until he is found. You have to remember, though, that maybe it wasn't your father at all."

"I don't know who else it could have been. As far as I know, Ryan didn't have any enemies at all. My father is my only known enemy. It had to have been him. I'm sure of that."

Brenda patted Lauren's hand and said, "There is a room around the corner from our apartment that we usually reserve for couples with small children. No one is in there now, and I'll take you to it so you can get some quality rest." Lauren asked if she could retrieve clothing and personal items from her room. Brenda started to agree and then she changed her mind. "Lauren, I'll get them for you. You may not be ready to see the room since it's still pretty messy. Tell me what you need."

Tears formed in Lauren's eyes. "Thank you, Brenda. I

really don't want to go back in there. Have they taken Ryan away?" Tears spilled uncurbed.

"He is not in there. Let's go. I'll take you to your new room." As they walked together, Brenda realized that Lauren still had not explained how her first boyfriend Seth played into this whole story and was determined to ask her as soon as she got the opportunity.

Before she could ask, however, Grace Mitchell emerged from her room just as Brenda and Lauren passed by. She told Lauren how sorry she was and gave her a quick, tight hug. "Is it alright to go downstairs for a cup of coffee, Brenda? I don't want to disturb the police," Brenda said.

Brenda was not happy to learn that gossip had spread so many details so quickly, but she supposed there was nothing much to be done about it. "Just be careful. There is still a lot of police business in the house. Get your coffee and then go back to your room." Grace readily agreed and sped off.

Brenda told Officer Swenson to stand outside Lauren's new room for protection. "No one is allowed to enter her room unless authorized, and right now no one is authorized other than Detective Rivers or me. This woman needs to get her rest." Officer Swenson took his station and Lauren looked relieved to have the protection of the police officer in front of her door.

Brenda retrieved everything belonging to Lauren from

her room and packed it all neatly into the woman's suitcase and overnight bag. They had talked enough for now, and she decided questions about Seth would have to wait. Instead, Brenda ordered breakfast to be brought up to Lauren's door and then told Officer Swenson to call her when the breakfast arrived.

The young officer stood outside the door with Brenda and told her a manhunt was going on outside. "No one but you, Brenda, would have discovered that hallway. You were lucky that man didn't take you out, too."

"Let's hope they find him soon."

"Is he really a madman?" At least Officer Swenson spoke in low tones.

"Just guard this door, Officer." He nodded and Brenda wearily returned to her office to take care of more details.

Inside the guarded room, Lauren knew she wouldn't sleep. Once she ate a good hot breakfast, she wanted to go over every detail of her life to this point in her head. She had never allowed herself to think much about the day her father was taken away due to her statement to the police. The aftermath of that terrible day had wreaked havoc on her life. Her father had retained an aggressive lawyer who, along with an unscrupulous but convincing psychiatrist, successfully swayed the court into believing that he was insane. Lauren had hoped he would be behind bars for the rest of his life. Instead, he got off easy, sent to a mental health facility that was in reality a mental hospital disguised as a minimum security prison. Once there, he walked the building freely, enjoyed three meals a day and all the medical care he needed, both physical and mental. The longer he was there, it seemed the less supervision he required. To Lauren, there was no other explanation as to how he escaped. The more she thought of the figure in her room in the dark, the more she was sure it was her father.

Now her dilemma was how to explain his presence at Sheffield Bed and Breakfast, many hundreds of miles away from Colorado. She paced the confines of the small room, hearing the police officer shift on his seat outside the door, thinking and worrying, the lack of sleep carving deep lines into her face as she waited.

Back in her office, Brenda typed up her statement about the confrontation in the dark passageway. She recalled the wild look in the eyes of the hidden man. It didn't prove he was Grady Fisher. Perhaps the killer was someone else who had a grudge against Ryan Meyers? The sight of the man with the knife could easily have triggered past events to rush through Lauren's head. The possibility that the young woman suffered from traumatic flashbacks was at the top of the list as well. She remembered the way Lauren drew back when Ryan pretended to stab everyone he passed in the room after his performance. No wonder she had recoiled at the role Ryan chose to play. Brenda didn't think Ryan Meyers would have chosen to be a zombie, much less pretend to stab everyone, had he known the trauma his wife experienced as a young teenager.

She stopped by Lauren's room and discovered that the traumatized woman still had not slept. She asked Lauren if she wanted something to calm her. Lauren felt the tension in her body was too strong and finally she agreed. Brenda called her own doctor and asked if he could prescribe something mild for her. She told Lauren to lie down while someone fetched it from the pharmacy, and she would be back soon.

By the time Brenda and Mac finished a light breakfast, Bryce's research had been completed and it eliminated any doubts about who the intruder was. On Mac's cell phone, Bryce called and spoke to them both as they sat in Brenda's office behind the front desk.

Detective Bryce Jones discovered that Grady Fisher had indeed escaped from the hospital. The institution had been searching for him for almost a week, but had never thought to look as far away as the Atlantic coast. The staff there did not know Grady's full criminal history, but after searching his room, they had found newspapers stuffed in the back of his closet that told the story of how he murdered his neighbor. The articles also noted how his own daughter witnessed the crime and had been the state's star witness against him.

Grady had been allowed access to the internet under

supervision in the mental hospital's small library. Later, one of the attendants admitted he perhaps wasn't watched closely when it came to his searches. They discovered many of his search inquiries included his daughter Lauren around the time she first met Seth Hill, and later at the time of her marriage to Ryan Meyers. He apparently had knowledge of her career, but more importantly, of her travels and adventures with Ryan.

"How did he get into that wall from outside?" Mac asked Brenda. "We haven't found him or a doorway."

"It has to be in the rock walls. Let's take a look downstairs near the kitchen area." Brenda told Mac about their chef's concerns. "He has heard scratching and we both thought possibly a small animal had gotten in. There has to be a place in the wall that leads to some stairs to access the other floors. Jolene King mentioned the first evening she heard noises from behind the wall. No one thought it was real and chalked it up to excitement about the Halloween spooks and ghost stories."

They left their unfinished coffee cups on Brenda's desk and headed for the kitchen. The detective asked specific questions of Pierre, who told him he had been hearing sounds on occasion for the past two days. Mac and Brenda stopped at the wall Pierre pointed to. Brenda began tapping against it in several places. When she heard a different sound behind it, she turned to Mac in surprise.

"It's here." She tapped again more aggressively, and the door slid open. She and Mac pushed it further until it was approximately as wide as a small closet door, then it stopped. Pierre's mouth gaped. Brenda glanced at him and told him to remember the area in case it locked behind them. She and Mac felt along the stone walls. Brenda turned her flashlight on, and, a few yards farther, they saw the narrow stairs they knew must lead to the second floor.

The silence enveloped them. The detective cleared his throat and stated he doubted anyone sinister was in the building now. Brenda whispered a reminder of how the man had blocked her in an instant. They crept to the top of the stairs until another wall stopped them. Brenda tapped until she found the metal bar that opened the narrow doorway into the second-floor passageway. Her flashlight shined ahead of them on full beam. It showed an empty hall.

"He must have snuck in during the daytime and hid in here," Mac surmised.

"If he was hidden in here for a long period of time, he could have become familiar with the house routines," Brenda said. "Perhaps he knew when no one was up here. But that doesn't explain how he got into one of the guest rooms?"

"He is smarter than we're giving him credit for," Mac said.

"Do you really think it was Lauren's father?" Mac stopped at her question. Brenda continued. "If Grady Fisher did kill Ryan, he knew exactly where he and Lauren would be this weekend and made his way here, from Colorado to the east coast."

"Then there is the question of how he knew about the secret passageway. I must check on the manhunt now, Brenda. Let's go back the way we came." Mac paused. "And why kill Ryan? Was it to punish Lauren?"

"That's what Lauren seems to think. But the true answer should be found in due time, Mac. Let's get out of here."

It was a relief to see bright sunlight again when they emerged into the kitchen, startling Pierre. Brenda apologized and began planning to seal all entrances to the hidden passageway as soon as this ordeal ended.

Deep in his hidden place, Grady Fisher thought back on everything that had brought him to this place. He had always assessed himself as the brightest person in the Rocky Mountain Medical Facility. He scoffed at the name of the place. Why didn't they call it what it was? He had been incarcerated in a true loony bin. The screams, night and day, drove him up the walls. Twice he tried to smuggle something sharp from the dining room after meals, and twice he was caught and watched closer than ever. If he could search for the screamers and kill them, he could be assured of sound sleep at night. Once he almost got away with it. Under the pressure of the watching nurses, Grady realized he needed a better plan, one that could get him out of that hateful place for good.

The nurses seemed to keep syringes handy and used them freely. After his attempts to steal table knives from the dining room, he learned firsthand just how freely syringes were plunged into unruly people. Grady often regretted instructing his lawyer to keep him out of the mainstream prison. He decided perhaps he should begin to act sane again. Over the years, he decided that in a regular prison, at least he would have a chance of appeals. He was sure he could convince a new judge and jury to discount the evidence of a deluded, angry fourteen-year-old teenage girl who thought she could get petty revenge on her father by throwing accusations around that she didn't understand. More than once, he wished he had turned her over to her aunt and uncle from the start. They'd wanted her from the beginning after his wife's accident. If he had relented, he wouldn't be where he was today.

He made up his mind to display only an even-tempered disposition and pretend to accept his living conditions, in hopes of gaining more freedom. It had taken several months and there were times he almost reverted to showing his deep-seated anger, but in the end, he managed to curb his instincts.

He knew when he won. It was the day the orderly in the library didn't hang over his shoulder watching his computer searches anymore. He pretended to be caught up with information about the Atlantic Ocean and its bountiful sea life. After a boring hour scrolling through hideously detailed pages about fish, the orderly left to take a snooze in the corner of the library, leaving Grady to his own devices.

If Grady Fisher had learned anything at all during his years in the hospital, it had been patience in order to get what one wanted. After a few weeks, he had full rein to search for whatever he wanted. He wanted to track his daughter most of all. He almost snapped when he discovered her Facebook page and read that she and her new husband Ryan were planning a trip to the eastern seaboard, a subject he now knew very well.

His distorted grin was a pleased one. He knew Sheffield Bed and Breakfast well by the time the day was out, having spent time looking up the historical blueprints online.

After the information about his daughter surfaced, he figured it wouldn't be hard to walk off the premises. He told a nurse that he wanted to take a walk outside. At first, she hesitated. If she didn't allow him to go alone, he planned to invite her along and kill her when they got to the wooded area that opened to his freedom. As it turned out, she agreed he could walk alone. She told him to be back in thirty minutes for lunch, but he knew that no one would check if he was there for lunch.

Grady had simply walked away through the woods, where he changed into stolen clothes. He caught a bus in the nearest town, using stolen money, and headed to the east coast before the mental hospital even knew he was gone. He would be out of the state before they thought to come looking for him. He would find his daughter before anyone could stop him. He would put everything to rights.

At that, Grady had smiled his first real smile in a long, long time.

Brenda headed upstairs to find Lauren. The officer outside her door told her he had not heard any sounds from the room in a while and he assumed Lauren still slept. Brenda knocked lightly on the door and called Lauren's name. The door was locked, so she slipped the master card into the slot, planning to simply retrieve the breakfast tray and check that the woman didn't need the sedative medication after all.

As soon as Brenda stepped inside, she sensed something was wrong. The muffled sounds coming from the bed caused her to hurry to Lauren's side. Tape had been tightly secured across her mouth and Lauren's arms and legs secured with zip ties.

That was when Brenda heard the security lock on the

door click behind her. The odor of stale cigarettes permeated her nose. The panic in Lauren's eyes told Brenda who the third person in the room was.

"You have confused my situation, Brenda," the low voice said.

When Officer Swenson heard the security latch click, he wondered why Brenda had locked the door behind her. The more he thought about it in the split seconds that followed, the more he felt certain something was amiss. He called out to Brenda and asked if everything was all right.

Grady Fisher flashed the sharp knife and stepped closer to the door. Menacing eyes told her not to make any false moves.

"We're fine in here, officer. Let Mac know Lauren is getting over her flu, please."

Grady took three steps toward Brenda and raised the knife in warning. She jerked back and bumped against the footboard of Lauren's bed behind her. Grady's low chuckle sent shivers through her.

"Unfortunately, I'm short on zip ties. Go to the closet and find a couple of wire hangers. I'm sure in a place like this you still keep wire ones like the old days." He pushed Brenda toward the closet and she numbly grabbed two thick wire hangers. She handed them to Grady. He sneered. "Pick again."

CHAPTER SEVEN

Lauren Meyers tried to draw her body into a protective ball. The restraints prevented this. She realized she had no choice but to remain in the position she was in. She tried to think of other things to still her heartbeat. Lauren was positive she would be her father's next victim. Thoughts of exactly how she would die weren't allowed in her mind. She felt lost in a fog of old memories, old grief and new grief, so that the fear of her own death was like a barely audible scream over the top of a cacophony of madness.

Brenda knew she had to stall Grady for as long as possible. She kept fit enough to think she could ward him off when the right moment arrived. He couldn't keep the knife in his hand and bend the wire hangers to secure her hands at the same time. Unfortunately, he had already thought about that.

"Now take the hangers apart, and make it quick."

Grady kept his eyes on Brenda and edged backward toward Lauren. With his back to his daughter, he gave her his message.

"I've waited for this day for a long time, Lauren. You threw your own father under the bus the day I killed Randy. You shouldn't have done that. Ryan didn't have to die. He didn't do anything to me, but you did. It's your fault the two of you switched sides in bed. I would never have stabbed him like I did."

Brenda slowly straightened one hanger. She read Grady's intentions. He planned to take care of Lauren first. The longer she stalled him, the better for Lauren, and herself. "How did you know which side either of them slept on?"

"I was in the room during the big shindig that evening. I smelled the pillows. She always used that perfume her mother liked." He became silent as if reminiscing on the past when times were better in the family. He gestured toward Lauren and the hard glint in his eyes returned. "Her mother's accident was her fault, you know. Did she snivel about that part to you too? Or only the part where her poor papa is the big bad villain?" He sneered again. "That's right. She begged her mother to let her go to some concert until her mother relented. She knew how to wear her down. She was on her way to pick Lauren up when the accident happened." He raised the knife above his head and waved it around. "My wife died! Lauren was the cause of it, it's true! She caused my life to reach rock bottom. Lauren caused everything bad that happened. She has to pay."

Lauren was trembling silently from her spot on the bed, terrified tears leaking from the corners of her eyes as she shook her head wildly in the negative.

Grady didn't seem to notice that Brenda had stopped unwinding the first hanger. Her only hope was to keep him talking and hope that her mention of Lauren's "flu" was suspicious enough to get the officer outside thinking. Also, Mac knew of the back door to this room that was always kept locked. She hoped it wasn't bolted with the double lock from inside. For the moment, she couldn't recall if it was or not, but knew if they had to shove through it, they could do so.

"What will you gain by killing Lauren? They're just going to put you away for murder. Haven't you killed enough people already?"

Grady seemed to realize Brenda was in the room, tearing his eyes away from his daughter. "After the first time, I knew it would be easy to keep at it until I killed the one who ruined my life. No one's life is of any value if it's possible to ruin a life the way my life has been ruined. We're all going to die one day. I merely hurry souls along. I've waited to come face to face with my betrayer, and here she is at last."

Lauren's eyes begged him to no avail. His attention was now fully on Brenda. "You're going too slow. Hurry it up or you'll be first in line." The knife blade glinted. "I let you go once, but don't count on my generosity a second time."

Brenda handed him the first straightened hanger. He ordered her to place it on the foot of the bed and hurry up with the second one.

Officer Swenson realized things were not going to plan inside the guest room. Until now, he'd heard only Brenda's voice. Then he was sure he heard a man's voice, which went up and down in volume. There was no doubt in the officer's mind that the voice was threatening...then there had been Brenda's curious mention of Lauren's flu. He could not remember anything being mentioned about the young woman taking ill, though he knew she had trouble sleeping. He called Detective Mac Rivers and told him quickly about his suspicions.

"I'm down at the waterfront, but I'll be there as soon as possible. I know Lauren doesn't have the flu. It must be Brenda's way of signaling something is wrong." Mac's heart beat fast as he raced back to Sheffield Bed and Breakfast with three officers trying to keep up with him. He still had Officer Swenson on the call and told him to go to the end of the short hallway and find the back door into the guest room. "There is one we keep locked that goes into a small storage area. It then connects to the room. Use your tools and get it unlocked. Break it down if you have to! My wife is in there with that madman, and so is Lauren! I'm almost there. Wait for me before you go inside."

Officer Swenson found the door to the guest room through the storage closet and turned the knob slowly. It was locked as Detective Rivers told him. He pulled out his multi tool and slipped it in to pick the lock. He heard the soft click that told him it was unlocked. After a few minutes, Detective Rivers reached him and motioned for him to stand back. He quietly turned the knob and opened the door. The others followed him inside the small cluttered storage room.

He heard Brenda's voice first. "Don't kill her. We can work things out."

"How will you do that? Do you think I want to go back to that loony bin? It's worse than prison. Someone is always hovering over you with a syringe, just waiting."

"It can't be too bad. Among other things, you are allowed to use the internet. Isn't that how you knew exactly where Lauren and Ryan would be this weekend? You had the opportunity to keep up with world events, too. You were fed three meals a day and had a bed to sleep in. You even got out enough to escape. It seems to me you had plenty of freedom."

He moved forward close enough that Brenda almost

choked when the foul cigarette breath swept her face. "You call that freedom? I'd like to see you sleep while mad screaming goes on around you night and day. I'd like to see you sleep easy when a nurse can come by with no reason and stick you with a syringe full of who-knows-what." He gestured around the modest room with its single bed which wasn't often rented out to guests, being more often used for extra storage. "Believe me, these accommodations are like a palace compared to where I've been living." The now familiar low growl turned sharper. "They watched me like a hawk until I made friends with one of the orderlies in the library. It took a while, and I knew I had to keep her on my side. She was gullible, and I won her over. She started trusting me and didn't look over my shoulder every time I got on the computer." His short laugh was hoarse. "She didn't follow the rules. Lazy. All of them were lazy, if you gave them enough time."

Mac edged closer to the unlocked door that led directly into the bedroom and listened. His body tensed as he waited for the right moment, trying to figure out the exact situation going on inside.

Brenda tried to disguise her footsteps as a stumble, using the move to inch toward the door that led out into the hallway. When Mac arrived, she wanted to be as far away from that storage door as possible. She only hoped and prayed the officers were actually waiting there to burst in. She was surprised they hadn't arrived yet.

"How did you know about the secret hallway?" Brenda asked. Her curiosity took over in the middle of the tension.

"I know every nook and cranny of this place. Years ago, it was an empty building with no purpose other than to fall apart. I was young then and free to do what I wanted. I had friends then." He jerked his head sharply toward Lauren. "She made sure no one wanted to be around me any longer." He focused on Brenda again. "I was young and single. A bunch of us decided to hitchhike out here and find an abandoned building to stay in while we had fun on the beach. We found this place." He chuckled and shook his head as if back in his youth. "We explored every nook and cranny of it. Jimmy, the oldest one of us, leaned against a wall downstairs and it opened up just like that. It was flimsier than it is today. We found that hallway and knew where it went. We stayed out here longer than we expected. It took a while to learn the whole place."

Brenda put the pieces of the puzzle together quite well after she heard his story. She took a short step backward and stopped. A few seconds later, she did the same until she was a few feet from the door to the hall. So far, Grady didn't seem to have noticed until he saw the near-intact hanger in her hand.

"Finish that hanger and then come back over here. Don't think you can escape out of here. I'm quick on my feet."

He raised the knife over his head. "I could kill her as soon as light came through the door and be out of here."

Brenda felt Mac was close by. She finished her task and put her plan in place. She held up the straightened hanger and lifted her chin defiantly. "If you want the hanger, why don't you just come for it, if you're so quick on your feet?" She smiled, and just as Grady Fisher stormed toward her, Detective Rivers and his officers rushed into the room.

Grady looked around, startled, and pushed Brenda aside. He turned the doorknob and realized it was locked. Fumbling to unlock it, he was too late. Mac swung him around and the knife flew from Grady's hand. Brenda felt the surface nick on her ankle and tried not to wince. She joined one of the officers who freed Lauren. The panic stood visible on her face.

"It's all right now, Lauren. We have him, and he won't hurt you or anyone again."

The frightened woman turned to watch as her father was handcuffed by several officers. "You don't know him. He's too clever. He could escape again from that hospital." Her voice bordered on a whimper.

"I don't believe he'll go to any hospital this time. There is nothing insane about him. Everything he has done has been thought out carefully and deliberately, even during his drunken rage when he killed your neighbor."

HIDDEN ENTITY

Mac yanked Grady Fisher to his feet. "Take him through the back way. We don't want to disturb our guests again." The two officers grasped the man in handcuffs and led him downstairs and out the back door to the waiting patrol car.

Brenda breathed deeply and then made sure Lauren was in good hands.

Clive Wilson sat in the enclosed back porch with his good friend William Pendleton. They watched the continuing scene in the rear driveway, the wild-haired man being guided into the police vehicle, which drove off without any lights or sirens.

"It looks like they got him," William said.

"I wonder why he stuck around inside the bed and breakfast?" Clive mused.

"There are plenty of places to hide in this big place. He had a reason. I reckon we'll find out soon enough. Brenda always fills Phyllis in on crimes she and Mac work on. We'll make sure we're right there when the story is told."

Clive relaxed. In spite of the gruesome murder of a guest, he somehow found it fitting that the whole thing happened at the spookiest time of the year, and with secret passages to boot.

"I do feel very badly about young Ryan Meyers. I wonder

what that other man had against someone like him?" Clive said.

"I heard Brenda mention she thought the killer made the wrong choice."

"Do you mean he meant to kill the lovely young woman?"

William shook his head solemnly. He smiled up at his wife who joined them. She had a coffee pot in her hand and refilled their cups.

"It's just terrible to think that murderer was hanging around here during the nice party. Who knows how long he was lurking back there? I wonder what he was doing all that time." Phyllis noticed Brenda coming in from the back door, watching as the squad car drove off. "Is that blood trickling from Brenda's ankle?" Phyllis said, aghast. She didn't wait for an answer and rushed to Brenda's side.

"I'm fine, Phyllis. It's quite a story, wait until you hear... I'm fine now, just shaken a bit."

"You're bleeding, Brenda," Phyllis protested. She stooped down to get a better look. "What happened to your ankle?"

"Grady's knife hit me when he was disarmed. Total accident."

"Who is Grady? Oh no, Brenda, you didn't try to confront the killer on your own?"

Brenda gave her friend a few spotty details and tried to reassure her, promising the full narrative once things settled down. Chef Pierre came out to the porch, hearing the commotion. He wiped his hands on his white apron and looked concerned.

"Don't tell me you got lost in that hidden passageway, Brenda. Wait, what's wrong with your ankle? I'll get a bandage for you."

Phyllis pulled on Brenda's arm. "There will be no waiting. You march over here and sit down while we get you cleaned up and you tell us exactly what is going on." Pierre returned with a warm cloth and a package of bandages. Brenda thanked him, and Phyllis helped her clean and take care of her wound. "Come on, Brenda. Tell us everything. I want to know what's going on with this so-called hidden passageway and who this mysterious Grady might be."

"I have to get back to Lauren very soon, but I suppose I can give you a few details." Brenda told them briefly of her two encounters with the killer. They were all mesmerized with the story of the hidden passageway behind the walls. "He seemed to be a very sick man. That's all I can say for certain. I can't give more details right now—not until the investigation is finished, or at least farther along. For now, all of you must keep this news to yourselves. I promise more soon."

When she returned to check on Lauren, she saw that the young woman had finally begun to relax.

"I need to be with normal people again, Brenda. I'd like to go down to the sitting room. It's time for afternoon refreshments, isn't it?" Brenda reminded her gently that she hadn't eaten since breakfast. Lauren insisted on going down, saying that refreshments with people around her would be a good antidote to the stress and the trauma of the long day.

A somber mood descended on the sitting room when Lauren entered, but Grace Mitchell and Karina Harris each hugged Lauren and expressed sympathy at the loss of her husband. Lauren thanked them and said she simply desired to enjoy some company. Clive, Phyllis and William joined them. They had been warned to keep conversation light, avoiding the topic of Lauren's ordeal. Phyllis poured Lauren a cup of chamomile tea to calm her nerves, but the woman only took a few sips before becoming distracted by the view out the windows to the Atlantic Ocean.

"We're going to take a walk down along the beach," Karina offered. "If anyone wants to breathe that wonderful salt air, feel free to join us." Lauren volunteered first.

CHAPTER EIGHT

J olene King caught up with Lauren and Karina
on the beach as they strolled among the swaying
dune grasses down to the sand and the waves.
She placed her arm around Lauren and pulled
her close. "I'm so sorry for everything, Lauren. I know
you thought me rude for asking about your connection
with Seth Hill all those years ago...but I wanted to let you
know, I've been thinking about him and I have something
to say. He must have been a weak man to have caved in to
his mother and abandoned you so heartlessly. He has no
idea what a strong woman you are."

For the first time in years, Lauren felt no pang in her
heart at the mention of Seth Hill's name. She only smiled
slightly at Jolene, musing, "Perhaps you're right. All I
know is that Ryan was the one for me all along." She
tilted her head upward and breathed the fresh air. "I still

have trouble thinking about my father as a murderer. For so long I suspected, but now I know the truth. He's vicious. He must have been happy to know I lost Seth due to his own reputation in the years after he went to the mental hospital. I'm sure it gave him great satisfaction. It's sad to think he wanted me to suffer as much as possible." She fought tears back. "I suppose what makes me the saddest is how much Ryan will miss out on. He'll never be the star performer he longed to be."

"Ryan showed a lot of talent," Jolene said. She thought from Lauren's conversation that perhaps it was cathartic to talk of her great loss. "Did he mean to go on stage one day?"

"I think he liked the idea of live performance, though he dreamed of one day being great, even being a movie star. His dreams were so vivid, even though he never took many steps toward them. I think he actually enjoyed the dream more than trying to make it a reality." She smiled through tears. "He was a real ham, wasn't he?"

Karina and Jolene laughed and agreed. "You know what would do you good, Lauren? A good old-fashioned dunking in the clean salt water of the ocean to help cleanse away your tears. We should go back and get our swimsuits," Jolene said.

Marcus came up behind them, picking his way carefully through the sand. "It is in the lower fifties, Jolene. No one swims this time of year."

"I know it, but it would be so romantic..." Jolene remained caught up in her vision, though Karina laughed it off, agreeing with Marcus. Lauren walked along the beach, thinking privately that her tears were enough salt for her that day, and was glad when Marcus finally succeeded in getting his wife to forget about the crazy plan.

Brenda was glad for the hundredth time that her guests took Lauren under their wings. She returned to the issue at hand. Lauren had given her the name of an older brother of Ryan's. It seemed he was the only one in his family who remained close to her husband. Brenda headed for the police station to join Mac so they could listen to the call together in his office.

As they both stood over the phone on speaker at Mac's desk, she placed the call to John Meyers to give him the tragic news. After he got over his initial shock, John asked a number of questions, including specific questions regarding the killer. Brenda attempted to calm him down when he spoke his next words.

"If I had known Ryan was marrying the daughter of a killer, I would have stepped in. Did he know his wife's father was a murderer? She should have told him. My poor brother. I'm sure if he killed this time, he has probably done it before."

"I'm sure any ongoing investigations will look for connections to the suspect, if there are any, but I don't know details like that. Lauren needs all the support you can give her right now. Do it for Ryan's sake. They were deeply in love, and that should be enough for you."

After Brenda ended the call, she turned to Mac, who was leaning in the doorway to the office. "Weren't you a little harsh with him, Brenda?"

"I suppose I was, to a certain extent, but it angers me that people blame her for her father's actions. That shouldn't happen. She can't control what her father does. Was she supposed to live a friendless, loveless life just because her father was criminally insane? Everyone could see how much in love they were."

The detective decided to change the subject. "Grady Fisher is waiting in the interrogation room. Will you join us?" Brenda readily agreed and followed Mac to the room. She had seen the arrest papers and saw the man was fifty-one years old. Chief Bob Ingram stood looking through the one-way mirror as the session began.

"You harbored a poisonous dose of anger inside you to do a thing like this," Mac said. "Why would you want to hunt down and kill your own daughter?" Mac waved his hand to stop the man when he started to give his pat answer. "I know all about her turning you into the police all those years ago. Spare me. I know that her testimony wasn't what put you in the loony bin. You got yourself there. From all reports, the police had plenty of evidence against you without her."

His demeanor shifted and became agitated, redness creeping up his wrinkled neck as he squinted angrily at the detective. "How dare you! You don't know me! How can you understand—" The clanking of ankle and wrist cuffs stopped him from standing up and flailing his arms around. Brenda and Mac leaned back and watched the pathetic show. It was then it seemed to dawn on Grady that Brenda was one of the interrogators.

"What are you doing in here? I've never known an owner of an establishment to interrogate suspects."

"Brenda is also an officer of the law in Sweetfern Harbor. Sit down and answer the question. Why did you try to kill your own daughter?"

Grady hesitated. His shoulders slumped, and he sagged against the back of the chair. His head lolled back on his neck for a second before he straightened a little, looking a bit saner than before. He seemed to consider for a second before starting again in a reasonable tone of voice. "Lauren was always a good kid. We were a happy family...until she killed her mother, my poor wife..." Mac stopped him again, slamming a hand down on the table angrily.

"She didn't kill your wife. She lost her mother that day. She was a child! She lost as much as you did, if not more, the day your wife had that accident. Lauren lost a mother, but she also lost her father's love that day, thanks to your way of twisting everything around. Get your head right! When do you plan to start blaming Grady Fisher?"

"I want my lawyer."

Once Grady was back in his cell, Mac took a deep breath and he and Brenda spoke with Chief Ingram. "We need to get the judge on this right away. Once his lawyer gets here, he'll try to get him back to the mental hospital," Brenda said.

"Maybe that's where he should be," Bob said. Brenda shook her head vigorously. She told the chief everything that had happened at Sheffield Bed and Breakfast in minute detail.

"I think he's a master of deception. He played the courts the first time. We can't let him play the courts again a second time."

"All right, I'll contact the judge right away," the chief said.

"There is plenty of evidence against him for the charge of murder," Brenda said, "But the judge might be even more convinced if we can just get one more thing. Do you think we can get a handwriting sample from him?" She explained the note, and Mac quickly left to retrieve the crumpled paper from the evidence box. "We're sure this note was written and left in the deceased's room by Grady Fisher," Brenda said. The chief read it and agreed they should proceed.

Back in Mac's office, Brenda sat deep in thought. "What's on your mind now, Brenda?"

"Something's bothering me. I have a sneaking suspicion that Grady killed the person he intended to kill."

"Where did that come from?" Mac said.

"Something Grady said to me when I found him that first time in the concealed passageway. He said he had very good eyesight. He said he had eyes like a cat, in fact—and that hall was so dark I could barely make out his features. So surely Grady knew it wasn't Lauren he bent over. I think he absolutely meant to kill Ryan and succeeded in that mission. The whole thing about trying to kill Lauren was fake—it was just play-acting. I'm not so sure he meant to kill her when he tied her up, either. It was all for show."

"What did he have against Ryan Meyers?"

"That's what I plan to find out." The detective had no doubts his wife would get to the bottom of this new, strange twist. Her eyes were already alight with energy as she said, "First of all, I'm going to research all I can about Seth Hill," Brenda said. "There might be a connection. What I know so far is that he comes from a very wealthy family. Perhaps there's a connection between him and Grady."

This time Mac failed to keep the laughter from his voice. "Grady Fisher was not a wealthy man, Brenda. As I understand it, he was a day laborer and went from job to job. Lauren grew up in a very working-class kind of household. That tells me he came across as...rough to a lot of people even before he started lurking with knives in secret passageways. I'm sure he had few friends before he ever killed his neighbor."

"You could be right about all of that, Mac. Perhaps Grady worked for the Hill family? I don't know. But I promise you I will find something explaining why he aimed for Ryan Meyers and not his daughter."

Mac knew to give her full rein, but he still doubted Grady Fisher was connected with Seth Hill, or Ryan Meyers, for that matter. Every time he had talked with the suspect, Grady merely repeated his calls for a lawyer, and while he waited, he certainly didn't let up on blaming his daughter for everything that had gone wrong in his life.

Brenda left the police station and drove to their cottage. She settled at her laptop while the water in the teakettle heated up. A good cup of tea by her side, Brenda settled in for a good search into the background of the Hill family. She discovered that Seth's family was wealthier than she had assumed. They were quite well known in the area where Lauren and Seth had grown up, contributing to many social and artistic causes and charities and appearing in the society pages frequently. Seth had one sibling, an older married sister who now lived in Europe. His parents did not seem to work and the more she read about their money, the more she realized that perhaps they were the type of people who had inherited quite a bit of money. The Hill parents remained very active socially, chairing gala events and hosting fundraising dinners for various town causes. Meanwhile, Seth carried on his father's real estate development business. Brenda spent several unsuccessful hours searching for any public records that might link Grady Fisher's name to the wealthy Hill family, but found nothing.

"Perhaps there are no records," she mused. "What if he was paid under the table, cash only? That might explain why there's nothing listed anywhere," she said aloud. Brenda paged through real estate records for the Hill family house, which certainly qualified as a mansion. It sat on twenty acres and was featured in a fancy photo shoot in a local magazine and an article all about the Hills' modest art collection and beautiful rose garden. Surely an estate of that size would have had dozens, if not hundreds, of laborers over the years.

She called Mac. "What else do you have for background history on Grady?"

"We don't have much. I take it you haven't found his name on the same page as Seth Hill's?"

She ignored the smile she heard in his voice. "I'm going to

talk with Lauren again. Maybe all my answers are right here at the bed and breakfast."

Brenda glanced at her watch. She had missed the afternoon get-together in the sitting room and discovered she was only fifteen minutes from dinnertime. A few of the guests, she knew, had checked out after giving statements and being cleared in the murder. The Kings, Clive Wilson, Karina Harris and Grace Mitchell were among those who would remain for another two days. Lauren Meyers asked to keep the apartment assigned to her for an extra day or two, which Brenda had told her was open for her needs for as long as she needed. She thought it best to wait until after dinner to have a long talk with Lauren about her life as a child.

However, when Brenda stopped by to visit her, Lauren Meyers told her she planned to skip dinner. "I don't have an appetite, Brenda. I was feeling so much better after a walk on the beach with some of my new friends I've met here—but now that I've been in my room alone, going through some of the funeral paperwork, the more it sinks in that Ryan is really gone." Her eyes began to well up. "I don't think I'll ever forgive my father for what he did."

Brenda reassured her quickly before the next onslaught of tears took over. "You can choose, Lauren. I hope you don't choose to let your father's actions rule your life. I'm sure it's not what Ryan would have wanted." She smiled reassuringly at her guest. "I'll call you later to see if you are hungry."

Brenda's plan was to have Chef Pierre make a light dinner tray with hot soup for her guest. She would take it to her after dinner, and it would be a perfect time for a chat. Satisfied, Brenda joined her guests in the dining room, where everyone sat to enjoy a hearty yet solemn dinner. There was muted discussion about Lauren's loss.

Towards the end of the meal, Mac joined the dinner guests so he could bring them up to date on circumstances. Brenda sighed with relief, and her guests perked up immediately at the prospect of gaining information.

"We have someone in custody for killing Ryan Meyers. We are waiting for formal charges to be arraigned, but I want to reassure all of you that the Sheffield Bed and Breakfast is a safe place to be. You are all safe. My officers are patrolling the neighborhood and the premises, both in uniform and in plainclothes, to ensure that no harm comes to anyone. I truly hope you enjoy the rest of your visit with us." When Grace attempted to ask a specific question, Mac told her he couldn't discuss details at this time. He enjoyed the plate of roasted chicken and vegetables that Brenda plated for him, but excused himself before dessert, saying he needed to get back to the police station.

Brenda met with Pierre as the dinner was being cleared

away from the dining table. He had no problem making the chicken and vegetable soup and was pleased to be able to help their guest who had suffered such a terrible loss.

Brenda called Lauren from the hall phone.

"I do feel a little hungry, Brenda, but please don't go to extra trouble for me." Brenda told her the tray was already ready and she would be up with it in minutes. Chef Pierre arranged a lovely tray with soup and a few freshly baked buns and a small pot of hot water next to several sachets of tea. Brenda climbed the rear stairs and brought it to Lauren's room.

"Let me help you get settled," Brenda offered, carrying it in and setting it down on the small table by the window. She removed the lid from the soup and the fragrant steam wafted temptingly toward Lauren, who immediately came to sit down.

"I don't think I realized how hungry I was," Lauren said, settling the napkin in her lap.

"I'm so glad we could help. Lauren...can I ask you a question?" Brenda waited until Lauren took the first sip of her soup and started to pour herself some tea. "Can you tell me about Seth Hill?"

Lauren stopped swirling the lemon ginger teabag in her teacup and looked at Brenda. "What do you want to know about him?"

"How long did you know him before he asked you to marry him?"

"We met while in college. It was a while before we started dating. I suppose because I worked so much—I had to earn money to get myself through college. He didn't have to do that, of course. His family had plenty of money. I always thought his parents disapproved of me and feared that he would dump me once we graduated since I wasn't really in his league. But we were madly in love with one another." Lauren's eyes shone with nostalgia. "Our love burned bright and fierce. We were convinced we were meant to be. Despite how different we were, there were so many coincidences in our lives that seemed fated. Our mothers had the same name, and we were born in the same month, in the same hospital, in fact. His father had lived in the town where I was born, though later they moved to a much nicer town; and apparently my father worked for the Hill family once, when Seth was very young." She took a sip of the tea. "That embarrassed me a little, actually, though Seth didn't seem to think it was weird. His father was a real estate developer, and mine just worked on a landscaping crew who redid his family's property." She laughed fondly and a little sad. "I guess he worked on the Hill property for several months. Seth never mentioned my father's crime. I really don't think he knew about that at the time."

Brenda kept her face utterly neutral when she learned

this latest information. "Did the Hills stay in touch with your father after that job? Did he go back there often?"

Lauren's eyes grew large as she thought back. "I do remember he did many jobs like that before my mother died. He liked working outdoors. But I have no idea who he worked for. I only knew that he'd done that landscaping job because Seth's father recognized my last name when Seth and I first started dating. I doubt very much that the Hills sought out my father or anything like that. After all, my father was a laborer, one of hundreds in that area, probably. Seth's family no doubt had landscapers and other handymen they worked with and never knew most of their names." She laughed self-deprecatingly. "I always did wonder how he could have fallen for a girl like me."

"He fell for you because he recognized quality of character, perhaps."

Lauren smiled but looked saddened. "His mother didn't agree with that, though. She knew the whole story about my father's deeds. I suppose I should have known it would be a matter of time before his circle found out and put it all together. After that, his mother was convinced that I was nothing but trash. It didn't matter what I was like—if I was related to a criminal, how could I possibly be good enough for her son?" Her face looked briefly contorted with bitter anguish.

"Did your father approve of Seth?"

Lauren became pensive. "Now that you mention it, when I told him I planned to marry Seth, his voice came across as the happiest he'd been in a long, long time. He hadn't been that happy since before my mother died. In fact, he was elated." Brenda pressed her to delve into his reasons, and Lauren thought carefully back while she took a few more bites of her soup. "It's a sad time to think about, but he barely kept food on the table after my mother passed away. My father drank every penny away. I had to steal money from his wallet sometimes just to buy cereal and bread, things like that. It was a constant source of strife between us. What was I supposed to do? Luckily, I had my own job in high school, which allowed me to have some money of my own, and then once I left for college, that was my true escape from the ruin that my father had made of our lives, especially after his heinous crime. Of course, I was still in contact with him sometimes...and then our old fights about money would start up again. Perhaps when Seth and I fell in love, my father thought I'd give him money just to keep him quiet. I remember him saying something about 'They won't like me coming around the Hill house' or something like that. Implying that I'd have to keep him a secret or he'd try to get out of the hospital in time for the wedding. I didn't think much of it at the time, but looking back, I wonder if money was the sick reason behind his behavior." She laughed softly. "He had spent years in the mental hospital by that time. I called him to tell him about Seth Hill, about our romance, and he was over the moon, but he also said some very strange things. I think it stirred up plenty of ideas that swarmed in his head." Lauren sat back in her chair and looked a little ill at the thought.

Brenda pressed Lauren's shoulder reassuringly as she stood to go. "You may be right about it stirring him up. Just don't blame yourself for anything he chose to do."

fter she left Lauren, Brenda met Phyllis and William in the back hallway. Phyllis buttoned her jacket and smiled at her friend.

"What's new, Brenda? Look at you with the color back in your cheeks—looks like you have recovered well from your ordeal. I am so glad you are all right," Phyllis said.

"Do you recall when I told you that I'd heard a cough behind the wall during one of my tours?"

"Of course, we remember. Why? Did you find a mysterious hidden door after all?" Both Phyllis and William laughed, but their laughter died when they saw the serious look on Brenda's face.

"You'll never believe what's been hiding behind the walls all these years..." Brenda told the Pendletons the details of her encounter with Grady Fisher and the subsequent confrontation between Grady Fisher and Lauren, leading to Grady's arrest. "I feel so sorry for Lauren. She's lived under a dark shadow most of her life, due to her father's crime. When she found Ryan, she was finally content and happy. Now she has lost love again and been betrayed by her father a second time."

Brenda updated her good friends on the latest pieces of the investigation. Phyllis was shocked and reassured her good friend, "We won't spread this around, Brenda. Is there anything I can do for Lauren?"

"There is an officer outside her door for a while longer. She wants to rest and be alone right now. I'll check later and let you know."

Brenda felt sure she had most of the puzzle pieces in place. The note Lauren read and crumpled after the room was ransacked began to make more sense to her. She grabbed her jacket and headed for the police station.

When she arrived, Mac was just putting on his coat, ready to finally end his long day. He was surprised to see his wife enter.

"Take your coat off, Mac. I have some things to tell you."

After she finished, Mac shook his head slowly. "I think you are on to something, Brenda. Let's go have another talk with Grady Fisher."

Grady mumbled something about being tired and ready

to turn in early when the officer on duty at the cells told him he was wanted in the interrogation room. "I thought I told you I wanted my lawyer," he grumbled when he was brought in. His ruddy features stood out more in the lighting than they had earlier in the daylight.

"Your lawyer will be here in the morning. But some new evidence has come to light and we want to give you a chance to set the record straight before it's too late, Mr. Fisher."

"How well did you know Seth Hill?" Brenda said.

He hesitated at first, and then twisted his fingers together. The silence spread through the room before he spoke. "A long time ago I did some work around his family home. He was just a kid then."

"Why did you keep in contact with him through the years?" Brenda said.

His eyes darted from side to side several times. "I didn't. Not until Lauren told me she was going to marry him…I knew she wanted to taunt me, but I was glad to hear the news. Even if it was just over the phone."

"Why?" Brenda kept her eyes on his until he lowered them. "Why were you so happy for her when you resented your own daughter so much? Every word you've said since you came in here has been nothing but blame for her. So why were you glad to hear that news?"

"That was one time when she made the right choice. Let's just say I needed things in that hospital that patients can't get unless they have the cash to bribe some guards and nurses. It's not cheap. And then there's the cash you need to buy the stuff—booze, off-label pills, any contraband like that. Anyway, I figured if her money troubles were over, I could just cozy up to her and she'd fork a little of that money over to me from time to time. Plus, I knew I would need more money, much more, when I got out of there. She was my meal ticket. With her getting that Hill family money, I could finally live the good life I deserved."

"So it had nothing to do with your love of your daughter; it was just that she would become your bank." Brenda was tempted to flick her pen in his direction but refrained.

He cracked a crooked grin. "She isn't very smart. She should have stood up to Seth's mother and fought for him. She really settled too low when she found Ryan Meyers later on. She would never have had a money worry for the rest of her life if she had married Seth. Seth loved her. I know that because when the engagement was announced, he actually called me and told me he hoped we could be friends even though I was locked up in that asylum." He repositioned himself in the straight-backed chair. "But I guess he changed his mind. I had a call from their family attorney next. A few hours later, a restraining order was presented to me. I was to have no contact with the Hill family and the big wedding was off."

Brenda was certain Seth Hill had not contacted the murderer. There was no reason to do so. It was obvious Seth found out about his crime and Lauren's role in the trial as witness to it. Brenda doubted Seth would have had anything to do with Grady Fisher. The tall tale about getting a restraining order from the Hill family attorney was ludicrous. She exchanged a look with Mac. They both knew that a restraining order would have no mention of a wedding in it.

Neither Brenda nor Mac spoke while he shifted again. The grin he displayed sent chills through both of them. "All that's behind us now. My little girl might have ruined my life, but now she can fix it. She doesn't have to worry about herself now, either. She's free to take Seth back and fight for him, like she should have done the first time around. He married someone else and then divorced. He's free as well. I don't expect to be in that madhouse much longer. Once I'm out again, my daughter will do whatever it takes to keep me as far away from her and her newly reignited love as possible—I'll get my piece of her substantial new-found wealth. I never intended to kill her. Why would I do that? I would have lost everything." He chuckled. "She just needed a good scare."

Brenda and Mac exchanged looks. There was no reason

to prolong the conversation or to try to tell the man that even if he was freed from the mental hospital, he could count on the rest of his days behind bars.

Once Grady was back in his cell, Brenda spoke. "I hope we can convince a judge to put him where he belongs. There is nothing crazy about Grady Fisher. He's a cold killer and nothing else."

"I think the same thing, Brenda. Let's go have a talk with Bob." Chief Ingram looked up when they entered his office, knowing what the two had to say before they said anything.

"Before you give me your assessment, let me tell you that I agree with you. He is not insane. He should be locked up for the rest of his life." Chief Ingram poured three cups of steaming coffee from a fresh pot he had brewed, knowing it was going to be a long night. They sipped in silence.

Lauren Meyers's cell phone rang on the bedside table in the bed and breakfast. She didn't recognize the number and chose not to answer. Whoever it was left a message. She heard the ping that signaled a new voicemail but didn't check it right away. She hoped calls from the press wouldn't begin again like they had after her father killed Randy.

Most of all, she longed to feel Ryan's arms around her again, to hear his laugh that signaled he was ready to put on a spontaneous show somewhere, or to simply sit near him and feel his presence close to her.

She plumped the pillows on her bed and reached for a book. Reading always took her far away and had been one method of coping in the past. She opened to the bookmark when the phone rang again. It was the same number, and she ignored it once again, annoyed.

Lauren knew she should listen to the first message or the calls would probably just continue. She pressed the button to listen to the message. Her heart skipped a beat when the caller identified himself.

"Hi, Lauren, it's me, Seth Hill. I heard about your husband's sudden death and want to express my condolences. I know it's been a long time...I just wanted to let you know I'm thinking of you. Perhaps we can get together sometime and have a good talk. I'm still in New York. If you like, I can send a car for you in Sweetfern Harbor. We can have lunch before you head home again." He left his number and email for her.

At first, Lauren flashed back to the time she fell in love with Seth. She recalled the fun they had and Seth's reassurances of his love for her. By the same token, she never forgot that it was his family lawyer who visited her in her apartment to give her the news that she wouldn't be marrying Seth. Bereft and heartbroken, she had not left her room for days. Seth hadn't reached out to her until an entire week had passed. Seth Hill was someone she told herself she never had any intention of talking to again. Yet she felt her heart beat faster wondering how Seth knew she was in Sweetfern Harbor. An uneasy feeling settled in the pit of her stomach as she considered the possibility that Seth had also stalked her over the years, just as her father had done. No matter what Seth's intentions, the idea was terrifying. She blocked his number from her phone and tried to concentrate on the novel. It wasn't long before she set it down, unable to follow the words on the page, and fell into a restless sleep.

The first person to come to her mind the next morning was Seth. She fumed, thinking of how smug he was to assume she would come running back to him. She had a funeral to prepare for. Or at least she thought so, until later that morning when she received an overnight, registered letter from Ryan's brother, John Meyers. In it he told Lauren he had remained executor of Ryan's will. He sent for Ryan's remains once the police and coroner were finished with their probing. Ryan was to be cremated, and John would take care of where the remains would go. The letter invited her to call him at a later date to arrange a memorial service for friends and co-workers, but otherwise left her with nothing to do.

Lauren sat on the edge of the bed. She felt nothing at this point. John may be in charge of what happened to his brother's remains, but she knew there was one thing she did have coming to her. Ryan had taken out a fifty-thousand-dollar life insurance policy on himself years ago, and she had done the same for him. She recalled how they joked that with interest, the money would grow over the years. They expected it to come in handy in their old age, not in their twenties.

The soft knock on her door startled Lauren. She asked who it was, and Brenda answered her. Lauren opened the door to her.

"I want to let you know your father asked to speak with you from his cell. You don't have to do that unless you want to."

"I doubt he feels any remorse. What does he want?"

"I don't know if he speaks the truth or not, but according to him, you weren't his intended victim at all. Ryan was who he intended to kill all along."

Lauren scoffed. She didn't hold back her disdain. "Why would he want to harm Ryan of all people? They didn't even know each other."

"He needs to tell you the whole story. He didn't tell Mac and me everything." Brenda looked closely at Lauren. Tears edged beneath her eyelids. "Is everything okay?"

"I just found out Ryan's brother is the executor of his will and he's having him cremated. I'll never know where his remains are."

Brenda glanced at the letter addressed to Lauren that lay on the dresser. "If he has that right, there isn't much you can do about it, I'm afraid. You will always have memories, Lauren. No one can take those from you." Brenda couldn't imagine the life Lauren Meyers had endured so far. She wouldn't blame her if she didn't want to speak with her father. "When did you last see your father face to face?"

"Before that horrible night right here, I hadn't laid eyes on him in twelve years. I didn't think I ever would again." She dabbed at her eyes with a tissue. "I'll shower and go see what he has to say. I'd like for you or Officer Sims to be in the room with me. I don't want to be alone with him."

"I can be there. I'll have an officer near the door, and you will be completely protected."

When Lauren was ready, Brenda personally drove her to the station, trying to reassure her she was taking the right step. She advised Lauren to take deep breaths as they approached the interrogation room where her father was waiting under guard. "Listen, but don't feel you have to speak. You can stand up and leave whenever you want to."

"I'm ready. This will be the last time I'll set eyes on him."

Grady leaned back in the chair when Lauren and Brenda

entered the room. His lawyer sat next to him, and Officer Swenson stood inside the door.

"Hello, Lauren." When Grady realized his daughter wasn't going to return the greeting, he shrugged his shoulders. "I freed you the other night, but I suppose you are as ungrateful as ever." He shuffled his feet in their chains and continued. "I suppose I gave you quite the scare. You deserved it, but I didn't plan to really kill you. I need you for better things."

Lauren held her eyes on the man but refused to speak.

"Ryan was never right for you. It was Ryan who took you from Seth Hill. He knew you were engaged to marry Seth and he just couldn't stand the idea. If he hadn't interfered, you'd still be with Seth today and I wouldn't be in this mess."

Lauren seethed. "Ryan didn't know Seth at all. I don't know where you got this outrageous idea, but you are wrong. He had never heard anything about him other than the fact that we were once engaged. Ryan didn't stop the marriage. Seth's overbearing mother took care of that. Of course, you're too selfish to understand that you were the real reason she was so against our engagement. You are the one who took Seth away from me, don't you get it? You and your sick, twisted crime. In a way, it all worked out against you. Ryan and I were very happy. For a time..."

"Surely your precious Ryan knew about my...incident with that poor, disgusting old neighbor of ours, Randy. Ryan must have put two and two together. You know, Lauren, you have never made good decisions and you blew it choosing Ryan over Seth. Seth could have paid for anything you ever needed or wanted in your life. What did Ryan Meyers have to offer?"

"He offered his love and it was enough for me. Your so-called incident was out-and-out murder." Lauren looked Grady in the eye. "Were you ever a happy person? Did you love my mother? Was her death just an excuse to become the weak, horrible person you'd always been inside?"

"You don't seem to remember how much time I spent with you and your mother. Doesn't that answer your question?" At Lauren's silence, he tried again. "Your mother...she knew who I was when she married me. Don't you get it? Maybe that's what killed her in the end, too. That's what sent her out on the roads so late at night in that icy weather the night of her fatal accident. She went looking for me at a bar, wanted to drag me home again. She thought she could change me," he spat. "Her accident was divine retribution. She deserved it. I was finally free. It's a pity you can't understand that. But then, you always were a bleeding-heart, just like her." His smile tugged cruelly at his mouth.

Lauren's face paled and her eyes were distant as she

stood up and walked past her father without a word. He watched her go with his legs sprawled out, leaning back as if ready to watch a favorite show, until the last moment when she slammed the door behind her with finality.

Once she came to a halt in the corridor, catching her breath, Brenda caught up with her.

"Ryan never knew Seth," Lauren said distantly. "He never connected me with my father and his crimes, either. If he had, it obviously didn't matter to him."

"It's horrible the things he said to you in there, Lauren. I'm so sorry. Surely it was his last attempt to twist your emotions and bind you to him. But it's time to go on with your life the best way you see fit. Think about setting up some kind of memorial in honor of Ryan, perhaps."

"That's a great idea, Brenda. That will keep me occupied." She stopped and looked at the sky filled with stars outside the police station's reception area windows. "This area is so picture-perfect, and so peaceful. It's the last place Ryan and I found happiness together, even if it was the site of the most awful tragedy that ended his life, it's also the place where I finally came to terms with who my father really is. It's the place where I finally got to see my father placed behind bars. Perhaps I'll rent a house around here and stick around until I figure out what to do next."

"You will find plenty of activities in the area to keep you

occupied. Have you ever tried sailing? It's very peaceful this time of year. The town is friendly, and I'm sure you will be accepted as easily as I was when I first arrived here."

Lauren took a deep breath. Ryan would approve. As for going forward without him, Lauren would have to figure that part out. She opted to walk back to the bed and breakfast alone.

Brenda watched Lauren walk away, her back straight despite everything she'd been through, and knew then that Lauren would find a way to begin her life again in peace.

Brenda returned to Mac's office. The detective slapped two folders down on his desk.

"I'm done for the night, Brenda. Let's go and do something that has nothing to do with crime."

"I'm all for that," Brenda said. "What did you have in mind?" Mac stifled a yawn. She laughed at him. "I see. It looks like you are ready for a long uninterrupted night of sleep."

The detective looked sheepish. "I'm amazed how astute you are, Brenda. Let's relax and do just that. I promise we can enjoy tomorrow doing something else."

"What about the clean-up? There's so much to deal with in the Halloween aftermath."

"There are plenty of young officers around to help take care of that. City officials will have their crews out on the streets, too."

Brenda thought he had a brilliant assessment of the situation and agreed the next day belonged only to the two of them. Hand in hand with the love of her life, she stepped out into the cool autumnal night and headed back to Sheffield House. The twinkling lights of the tiny oceanside town winked in the evening air, and the bright moon, high in the sky, followed them all the way home.

ABOUT THE AUTHOR

Wendy Meadows is the USA Today bestselling author of many novels and novellas, from cozy mysteries to clean, sweet romances. Check out her popular cozy mystery series Sweetfern Harbor, Alaska Cozy and Sweet Peach Bakery, just to name a few.

If you enjoyed this book, please take a few minutes to leave a review. Authors truly appreciate this, and it helps other readers decide if the book might be for them. Thank you!

Get in touch with Wendy
www.wendymeadows.com

amazon.com/author/wendymeadows

goodreads.com/wendymeadows

bookbub.com/authors/wendy-meadows

facebook.com/AuthorWendyMeadows

twitter.com/wmeadowscozy

Made in the USA
Columbia, SC
09 February 2021

32663659R00085